About the Author

Martina Adovica is a writer originally from Riga, Latvia. She grew up in Luxembourg and spent several years studying law in Glasgow, Scotland, a city which stole her heart. She currently lives in Luxembourg with her two cats, Sunny and Mooncake, and is working on a novel.

The Clothes I Never Wear

Martina Adovica

The Clothes I Never Wear

Olympia Publishers
London

www.olympiapublishers.com
OLYMPIA PAPERBACK EDITION

Copyright © Martina Adovica 2024

The right of Martina Adovica to be identified as author of this work has been asserted in accordance with sections 77 and 78 of the Copyright, Designs and Patents Act 1988.

All Rights Reserved

No reproduction, copy or transmission of this publication may be made without written permission.
No paragraph of this publication may be reproduced, copied or transmitted save with the written permission of the publisher, or in accordance with the provisions of the Copyright Act 1956 (as amended).

Any person who commits any unauthorised act in relation to this publication may be liable to criminal prosecution and civil claims for damage.

A CIP catalogue record for this title is available from the British Library.

ISBN: 978-1-80439-966-8

This is a work of fiction.
Names, characters, places and incidents originate from the writer's imagination. Any resemblance to actual persons, living or dead, is purely coincidental.

First Published in 2024

Olympia Publishers
Tallis House
2 Tallis Street
London
EC4Y 0AB

Printed in Great Britain

Acknowledgements

Publishing a book has been a dream of mine for as long as I can remember so I wish to thank every single person who has had to listen to me ramble about my stories and my ideas for a book. More importantly, I want to thank my family for always inspiring me and supporting me. I would not be who I am without you. I also want to thank my closest friends who have read my stories, provided feedback, kept me motivated whenever I wanted to give up and who have been there throughout this entire journey. You know who you are. Finally, I want to thank my cats for trying to contribute to these stories by walking across my keyboard while I was writing some of them.

Mechanisms of Loneliness

1

It was the fifth night in a row of pan-fried potatoes for dinner. Evie sat at the table staring at her father's serious expression as he tried to assess whether they were cooked all the way through. The television sounded in the background as the final moments of yet another episode of the daily Venezuelan soap played out just before the news would come on. The flat was filled with many sounds, from the voices coming from the TV and the oil jumping out of the pan to her brother playing music in the next room.

'Luke, time for dinner,' her father called out as he started distributing the potatoes on three plates, while Evie added some salad on the side.

He was doing the best he could. His cooking skills were incredibly limited, however, rather than order take-aways or buy something already prepared to diversify their meals, he still wanted to cook because he was adamant that they should always have a home-cooked meal.

When her mother left, he spent weeks trying to pull himself back together. The three of them quickly realised that he did not know how to do the most basic tasks. As a result, he would often have to call her and have her explain how to do certain things, such as how to use the washing machine properly. However, some things he just couldn't hang of, try as he might. Evie's mother had always sent her to school with her hair tied up in a high and sleek ponytail, and although he attempted to do this, it never looked right. Because of that, he always took her to school early and had one of Evie's teachers get her long hair made up the same way just so he could maintain some semblance of a normal routine.

Her father liked routine. They would always get up at half-past six in the morning on school days so that he would have time to do his daily crossword while Evie watched this process attentively, chomping down on her breakfast cereal next to him. On weekends, he would always get up at ten past nine, without the aid of an alarm clock. If Evie was ever up before him, she just lay in her bed and listened to the first sounds of her father getting up and going to make coffee. Him having those moments of solitude on those mornings was a crucial part of the routine, and she did not want to impose on that.

Drinking had also become part of this life they led. Every evening, once they had all had dinner, her father would open a beer bottle, which then turned into two and then three. When Luke and Evie had already gone to bed, she could still hear him bustling about in the living room. At the time, the saddest sound Evie could think of was hearing him open the freezer and the noise of the bottle of vodka gliding against the ice as he took it out. She didn't know how much he drank, but she knew that it was his way of coping, and so sometimes, when it all got too much, he drank more than he should have. Sounds of him throwing up in the bathroom were a weekly occurrence. Yet he still went to work the next day as if nothing had happened.

They never discussed her mother leaving. They had never really talked about anything that mattered. Conversations were limited to questions about schoolwork, plans to go to the store or him having to take her to or from a friend's birthday party, or her father's favourite topic of all – the weather. He constantly checked a Norwegian application that he had downloaded on his phone, and whenever there was an awkward moment of silence at home, a mundane weather update seemed to be just the thing to break it. This was taking its toll on the three of them. Thankfully, Evie and Luke sometimes talked about it as they sat and played video games in Luke's room. Discussing it even for a moment helped lessen the pain. However, Evie's heart ached when she realised that while she at least had Luke to talk to, her father had no one and he wanted to keep all of that pain to himself and deal with it alone. Although her mother had gone abroad to work and the two of them had not split up, she had done so without even considering that the three of them should move there with her. She would come back to visit every few months when she could, but those moments with her seemed to pass so quickly that Evie could hardly remember what exactly they had done when she was here. All Evie had as memories were the souvenirs she had brought with a foreign language sprawled across every single object, making it feel distant and unfamiliar. She wanted to confront her father about her worries and to ask him if there was even the slightest chance of her coming back for good, but this seemed impossible.

  Every Thursday morning, Evie's school day started an hour later than usual so, after dropping off Luke at his high school, she and her father would go to a petrol station where he would fill up the car and buy her a diet coke and a Bounty and they would sit in the car, while she ate the candy bar and he drank his second cup of coffee of the day. Every single Thursday, Evie thought that this would be the moment when she would finally be brave enough to talk to him about something meaningful. Yet, it never happened. Instead, they turned on the morning radio show, and her father listened attentively to the weather forecast.

Sunday was Evie's favourite day of the week as they would often do things together as a family. Whether it was going to visit her grandparents or going to a nature park for a walk, those days always felt more normal than others. Once their activity for the day was out of the way, they got back home and made dinner, which was always grilled salmon, rice and salad. This was a welcome change after a week of potatoes. Luke often stated that he was on the verge of not eating dinner any more because it had become so tiresome but, despite the many times that he said this, he still joined them every night. Dinner was followed by sitting down in front of the television. Sunday night was dedicated to whatever singing competition was out at the moment, so the three of them could comment on how bad the show was or judge the competitors, which Evie considered to be the epitome of family bonding. Yet, whenever there was a particularly good singer or when someone had a truly emotional story to tell, her father would often burst into tears. At first, she had tried to comfort him, but she soon realised that it wasn't about the show. This was the only moment in which her father let himself be vulnerable, and so neither Luke nor Evie wanted to disrupt that. Therefore, they just sat there, staring at the images moving on the screen, while their father was sobbing next to them.

On one of those Sundays, after spending the day at their grandparents' house and stuffing themselves with pancakes, Luke and Evie were playing a videogame together while their father did the laundry. Evie was trying her best to imitate a sports commentator as Luke played football and, even though she was terrible at it, Luke nevertheless appreciated her effort. However, he seemed more downcast than usual, and Evie was waiting for the right moment to ask what was wrong but, before she had the chance to, he came out with it himself.

'I overheard a conversation between Mum and Dad yesterday.'

'Is she going to visit soon?'

'In a month, I think. But I heard them talk about how you would be moving over there to live with her.'

'Just me?'

'Just you.'

2

After giving her a quick kiss on the cheek, her mother was out the door. While Evie had only been living with her mother for two months, she had noticed that her mother went out quite often. Evie rushed to the window and peeked outside. The neon sign of the bar below cast a raspberry light out onto the street, the water on the pavement glistening in pink tones. Her mother appeared, coming out from the building and heading for a car parked only a few steps away. Evie's eyes widened as she saw her get into the car and kiss the man sitting in the driver's seat before they drove away.

    She sat on the side of her bed, hands crossed across her body, shivering slightly. It felt as though her mother had betrayed them. The time that the three of them had spent longing for her and thinking that her mother felt the same pain of missing them now felt tainted since her mother had obviously been busy constructing an entirely different life of her own. Evie knew that she might still have a place in it, but her father did not. She did not know what to do with herself, so she just turned on the TV and stared blankly at it. Her zombie-like state was interrupted by the sound of the landline ringing. It was her father. He was slurring his words and she could tell that he was crying.

    'Is Mum at home?'

    'No, she went out.'

    'Where did she go?'

    'I think she went out to a concert with her friends from

work,' Evie said, loathing herself for lying, but she just couldn't bring herself to hurt him with the truth.

'Pet, I miss her so much.'

'I know. She misses you too.'

'Does she?'

'Yes.'

'Has she—' He paused, and Evie was sure, she could hear him take a sip of his drink. 'Has she been going out with another man? Has there been someone around?'

'No.'

Her father started crying harder and with that and Evie knew that she had been unable to lie convincingly.

'Why is she doing this?'

'I don't know, Dad,' Evie started crying too. She sat down on the floor, clutching the phone, feeling her eyes sting from her tears. 'Dad, is Luke with you?'

'He's out.'

'Promise me you won't drink too much and that you'll be okay,' she said.

Her father did not say anything, and so Evie repeated this.

'I'll be okay. I promise. I'm sorry, pet. I'm so sorry. I should go. Go to sleep, okay?' Evie nodded, even though her father could not see her. After he hung up, she went to wash her face and got into bed. As much as she resented her mother for causing him so much pain, she couldn't stay mad at her because Evie loved her too much. She also knew that she could never confront her mother about this, feeling a sense of *déjà vu* overtake her.

*

The days passed quietly but with effort. Evie went to school and was forced to deal with issues that come with being the new kid. Therefore, when she came home, she just hid in her room and tried to clear her head, ignoring whatever her mother was up to.

Yet one day, upon coming home, she heard voices as soon as she opened the door. When she went into the living room, she saw her mother and the man from the car sitting at the dining table with coffee cups and pastries before them. They looked truly happy. When he saw Evie, the man stood up and walked over to her.

'Hi, you must be Evie. Your mum has told me so much about you.'

Her mother smiled and gestured for Evie to sit down. For a moment, there was silence until the man started talking. Her mother finally put an end to his rant three hours later and made him leave. The whole time, Evie had hardly heard a word since she couldn't stop focusing on how sloppily he was eating his *pain au chocolat*; the pastry flaking and falling on his shirt. The only things that Evie could remember from this tsunami of words were that his name is Peter, that he likes music, perhaps too much, since he kept name-dropping obscure musicians who Evie had never heard of, that he thinks her mother is the most beautiful and intelligent woman that he has ever met and finally that he was looking forward to all of them going on a trip to Paris together. This last detail had alarmed Evie, yet she stayed silent until he had gone. Before she could say anything, her mother had read the expression on her face and assured her that this would be a great opportunity for Evie to get to know Peter and that she would love Paris. While Evie remained unconvinced, she decided to pretend that she was fine with this, although by keeping the anger that she felt inside of herself, she felt as though she was betraying her father.

*

The following Friday, Peter came over in the evening as they were due to set off for Paris the next day. Muffled sounds of laughter pushed through the door into Evie's room, entirely unwelcome. While her mother and Peter had dinner and drinks in the living room, she had attempted to paint as a way of distracting herself. When that failed, she organised her entire room for the third time that week and packed for the trip. Once that was done, there was little else to keep her occupied, so she watched a few episodes of *Buffy the Vampire Slayer* and sighed at the thought of not having such a secret, something that would make her special and interesting. She just had to go to school as herself and be an outcast without having anything to make up for it. As she drifted off into these thoughts, she suddenly heard a commotion outside her door. She peeked through the keyhole and saw her mother hitting Peter with a broom, apparently trying to get him to leave. He was trying to avoid her attempts at poking him as best as he could, and he finally got hold of the handle of the broom, pulling it out of her mother's hand. Peter then pulled her towards him and kissed her passionately, unleashing a wave of compliments her way, after which they walked off towards her mother's bedroom. Evie was so disturbed by this scene that all she could was go back to her bed and try to fall asleep.

The following morning, Evie closed the hood of the moss green car, squinting her eyes from the small drops of rain that were violently falling on her face. As she opened the door to the backseat, she noticed a pile of CDs stretching across all the seats with some on the floor of the car, along with mysterious leaflets and three different umbrellas. She pushed it all to one side and sat down behind her mother, putting on her seatbelt and holding on to her rucksack, which was shaped like an elephant, because that seemed to be the only familiar thing in this whole mess. Evie's pedantic nature made her feel repulsed by the disorder that she was sitting next to, but, more than that, it hurt her that he had not even thought to tidy it up, knowing full well that she would have to sit there on their way to Paris. In her eyes this was a reflection of Peter's entire personality.

The trip there was fine as Evie fell asleep only a few minutes after they had started their journey so that she awoke when they were already driving down the boulevards, the couple trying to find their hotel.

They went out for dinner the first evening, and as they walked along the old streets of the Left Bank, Evie pretended that she was there by herself, having already fallen in love with this city. Even though the trees had lost their leaves, as they lay wet and crumpled on the pavements, and a cold fog hung over the buildings, this was the most vibrant and beautiful place that Evie had been to. They found a restaurant and had dinner there and, while Peter and her mother talked, Evie just stared through the window at the passers-by on the street. She played a game where she tried to guess which people, particularly women, were tourists and who were real Parisians which turned out to be surprisingly easy. The women had a carefree elegance in their way of dressing and how they walked, which Evie decided to strive to imitate once she was older. In the background, she heard Peter trying to explain to her mother why he had chosen the wine that they were having for dinner as this was more so a wine for women rather than men, which is why he thought that she would like it. Evie inconspicuously rolled her eyes, and her mother proceeded to tell him that this was a silly and utterly non-existent distinction, which they continued to argue about for quite a while.

This squabble carried over to the next day but was soon replaced by another one. The whole day seemed to pass in a loud buzz as they explored museums and small shops and, while Evie felt completely alone, she also felt the painful sting of a headache from the constant tirade of arguments. It was late afternoon when they made their way back to the hotel before dinner, and they stopped at a supermarket to buy some water. As they walked along the aisles, Peter remembered that he had not brought deodorant with him on the trip. They bought all that they needed and returned to the hotel to rest their legs before setting out again for an evening walk. An hour later, Evie and her mother were waiting in the hotel's vestibule, ready to go to dinner. Peter soon joined them but told her mother that they must stop at the supermarket where he had bought his deodorant because the aerosol can didn't work properly. Evie tried not to laugh, but she saw her mother's incredulous stare turn to anger because neither of them could understand why he wanted to bother with returning something which he had spent less than four euros on. Visibly upset by this, Peter began explaining the value of things as they left the hotel and began searching for restaurants. This once again turned into an argument that made Evie try to walk quite a way ahead of them to avoid listening to their frustrations.

They were in the middle of the Boulevard Saint-Germain, when the two of them started raising their voices so that passers-by began to take notice. They had stopped and, as Evie stood to the side and observed the scene, she thought to herself that it seemed even more bizarre than anything that she had ever seen in films. Her mother and Peter were arguing, quite animatedly, waving their arms around. While they were trying to raise their voices, their words still came out as whispers, perhaps as they wanted to avoid drawing even more attention. This whisper fight seemed surreal to the point where Evie began to wonder whether she had just lost her hearing after having listened to them for the entire day. Yet the cars passing by on the street sounded as they normally did, and the cafés were buzzing with conversations, drinks and light-hearted fun. In just a few moments, Evie was forced to leave that inviting atmosphere behind.

Only an hour later, they were on their way back home since her mother had refused to stay there for another day as she said that her trip had been ruined. Once Peter dropped them off at the door of their building, he tried to apologise, but her mother closed the door in his face.

*

Only a few days later, her mother was once again out, and Evie was speaking to her father on the phone. He had drunk too much and had called with the hopes of talking to her mother. This had become such a regular occurrence that Evie now spoke to her father more than they had ever spoken to each other when they were still living together. It had become their routine.

'Why don't you just come and visit us?' Evie said, twisting the phone cord around her hand. 'You could show up without telling her, like in some movie.'

'I can't do that, pet. She wouldn't like it.'

'Maybe that's just what she's waiting for. How do you know that if you haven't even tried?'

'I can't, Evie, that's just not me.'

As her father was about to ask her something about school in order to change the subject, there was a ring at the door.

'What was that?'

'Someone's at the door.'

'Go and see who it is, I'll wait.'

Evie went to check and saw that the call was coming from the lobby. Through the camera, she saw Peter. Since she had been convinced that her mother was out with him, this took her by surprise. She stared at the pixelated man before her and knew that nothing would convince her to let him in. She went back to the phone.

'It's someone I don't recognise, so I'm just going to ignore them.'

'Smart girl.'

Evie kept talking to her father, and although Peter continued to ring the bell for a while, he eventually stopped. When her mother got back home, Evie told her that he had been here, looking for her.

'Poor guy. He'll soon give up, I'm sure.' This was all she said before heading off to sleep.

*

One night, as Evie was lying in bed, trying not to fall asleep since she was dreading going to school the following day, she couldn't help but hear her mother in the living room, singing along to Gloria Gaynor's *I Will Survive*. She kept replaying the song, and finally, Evie was sure that she could hear her crying, so she got up and quietly tiptoed to the living room. Her mother was sitting on the sofa, her cheeks covered in mascara, tarot cards laid out before her and a glass of wine in her hand.

'Mum, are you okay?'

Her mother immediately swiped at her tears. Evie walked up to her and sat down on the sofa, giving her a strong hug.

'Is this about Peter?'

'No, we've ended things, but I couldn't care less.' She paused. 'Evie, never fall in love. It never ends well. It's nothing but pain because whenever you fall in love with someone, it's guaranteed that they will never love you back.'

'What about you and Dad?'

'I haven't been in love with your father for years. And now he loves me. The irony of it all,' her mother laughed. 'When we first met, I thought that he was the love of my life, but then only a few weeks after we were married he cheated on me, and I haven't been in love with him since. If I had not been pregnant with your brother, I would never have stayed with him then.'

Evie was silent for a moment because she did not know what to say to that. Her mother saying this had cast a shadow over her entire childhood, over all the times that she had felt happy that she had such a loving family and parents who were meant for one another.

'Never reveal your true feelings to a man and never admit how much you like him because men feed on that.' At this point, Evie was incredibly surprised that her father and her mother had come to know one another, let alone fall in love since both were so clearly opposed to communicating their feelings to other people.

'Then who are you talking about?' she finally said.

'I've been seeing someone I met through work, this very handsome Greek man. He's just acting the way I knew he would, but I really deluded myself into believing that he wouldn't. I'm so in love with him that I think I'd do anything for him, but now he won't even speak to me.'

Evie never even met the Greek because very soon after this came Julian.

*

Julian was younger than Peter and more down to earth, yet Evie didn't like him from the first time they met, which was just as she got home from her dance class and he was on the verge of leaving the apartment. Her mother stood in the hallway in her silky bathrobe and smiled at him as he winked at her before closing the door behind him. Evie did not ask any questions and just went to her room. He came around quite often for about a month before moving in to live with them. Her mother mentioned that he had very little money and had spent what he had on a complicated legal battle with his ex-wife, which was still ongoing.

The two of them went out very often, and she could see that this made her mother weary because she had become less enthusiastic about leaving the apartment. Even when Julian and her mother weren't at a bar or café but just spent the evening at home, Evie felt like she never had the chance to talk to her mother without him lingering beside her. He was stuck to her from the moment she made breakfast to the moment that the pair of them brushed their teeth together at night. By this point, Evie was so used to being alone that it did not matter that much, however when her mother had been with Peter, those nights that she was at home in the next room and not somewhere with him, Evie had still felt like a part of her mother was hers. That was no longer the case.

Months passed like this. The two of them alienating one another more and more, with this man standing between them. Spring was starting to take over as cherry trees bloomed, the noise from the bar below became louder each night, and Evie eventually caught a cold. Her mother let her stay at home and for

Evie spending the day at home was heaven, as she could just watch *Angel* for the entire day and avoid all the people who constantly picked on her. As she munched on donuts for lunch, she heard the sharp sound of the landline at the door, calling from downstairs. She went to look at it and saw two men, who she had never seen before. She picked up the phone and quietly asked who it was.

Everything happened very quickly after that. She opened the door, they came up, along with two other women and a young man in uniform and started searching the flat. Evie called her mother, who was at the house in ten minutes, watching them work through each of the rooms. The senior inspector assured her that although an allegation of theft had been made, they knew that it can often turn out to be nothing in such divorce cases. Which it did. They did not find the money, phone and laptop that were alleged to have been stolen by Julian from his ex-wife, but the police said that they had probable cause to arrest him, given that he had broken the restraining order that she had obtained against him by showing up at his ex-wife's workplace earlier that day. Which, granted, had been because she had called him to tell him that she had informed the police of the alleged theft, and he had been furious because he adamant that he was innocent, but the circumstances did not really matter. That would be decided by the court. Julian was now in custody but would soon be transferred to a kind of holding facility for minor offences.

As such, the following Saturday, instead of going grocery shopping with her mother and then going back home to watch one of her many favourite television series, Evie sat in a car in the parking lot of that prison facility, while her mother went in to visit him and to bring him some cake because it was his birthday. The same was true of the Saturday after that and all the ones that followed it for the next three months until the judge heard his case and released him. Meanwhile, her mother had already moved on to someone else.

Evie didn't know who it was because she could tell that her mother was for once slightly embarrassed that she was already seeing someone new. However, by now, it had become clear that her mother could not live without a man by her side so, whatever the reason for that may have been, Evie was not surprised by this turn of events.

When Julian returned home, her mother spared his feelings for merely two days before letting him know that he would have to move out. The scenes that followed were both terrible and heart-breaking, but Evie refused to pay attention to it all. Whenever even a hint of an argument could be heard from the other room, she put her earphones in and disappeared into another world. This went on for months before Julian finally moved out. He had been sleeping on the sofa in their living room for all that time, and on the morning that he moved out, he did so without even waking Evie and her mother, disappearing as if he had never been there to begin with.

Yet the fact that Evie had disassociated from the world came at a price. As the only phone in the house was in the living room, her father's nightly calls went unanswered, and so she had not spoken to him for months. She had written emails to him, but his answers were always the same since he mentioned the weather, how busy he was at work and which reality show Luke and he were watching. Even though it was difficult to admit, Evie missed his drunk calls because, for once, she had been able to feel close to her father and get a glimpse of his true character. However, it seemed like that moment had passed and that she would have to accept that her father would become a stranger again.

*

The air was hot and dry. Walking towards her apartment building, Evie felt her face sting pleasantly from the slight sunburn that she had acquired. She was smiling to herself. Evie had been to the park after school with one of the girls from her class. The two of them had formed a friendship because they were both outcasts, and she could not have been happier about it because it was such a relief to finally have someone in her life who she could talk to. The pair had bought McDonald's and ate cheeseburgers and fries in the playground of that park while sitting at the top of a high platform leading to a giant slide, enjoying the sunshine and talking for hours. Although Evie didn't mention anything about what was going on with her parents, talking about people from school and especially the boys that they liked already made her heart feel a little lighter.

Upon getting home, Evie knew that her mother would be surprised that she had been out for so long, although it was only eight o'clock in the evening. However, when she opened the door to the flat, it was silent and dark. Evie knew that her mother should have been back from work by now, and so she walked from room to room, seeing if her mother had left a note saying that she had gone out. However, there was no note and there were no messages from her on their phone. Then, upon passing one of the small tables in the living room, Evie noticed that there was money on it and quite a substantial amount at that. Her mother was never as careless as that with money, so the fact that it was there sent Evie into a panic. She sat down on the sofa, the bank notes in her lap and after a moment tried calling her mother. Call after call went unanswered, and finally, on the seventh call, a robotic voice told Evie that her phone was out of reach.

The thoughts that rushed through her mind terrified her, so she could only sit in the dark and let the panic overtake her. She was convinced that her mother was dead. If not that, then Evie at least hoped that her mother had managed to somehow escape and run away from the threat that she faced and had left this money so that Evie could make her way back to her father. She did not know which of her many men could be responsible for her mother having to flee, but since Evie had never really liked any of them and did not even know who her latest lover was, this scenario seemed entirely plausible. Evie thought about when it would be appropriate to call her father, how she could buy plane tickets as an eleven-year-old girl or how she would even get to the airport. Maybe her mother had intended for that money to be spent on food while she waited for her father to come and get her. This indecisiveness paralysed her and kept her sitting in the same position for hours. She watched the minutes go by on the clock above the TV, and two hours later, she heard the distant sound of a key being turned in the door. She rushed to see who it was, hardly feeling her legs as she stood up. When she saw her mother turn on the light in the corridor, Evie stopped and burst into tears at the sight of her. She leaped into her arms, hugging her so strongly that she feared her mother would burst and disappear again.

'What's wrong? What happened, pet?' Her mother kissed the top of her head and held her close.

As Evie explained what she had thought happened through sobs, her mother's eyes turned glassy, and in mere moments, the two of them were crying together. Her mother explained that she had put that money aside to pay the workers who were to paint the kitchen the following week. Something that she had mentioned in passing one morning, but Evie had forgotten. However, more importantly, sitting in that corridor, her mother promised her that she would never do anything that would make Evie even believe that her fears were a possibility.

She kept her word.

3

Evie lay on her side, eyes wide open, Ben's hand limp across her body. She was staring at the blue light coming from her phone while messages silently appeared on the screen one by one. They were probably from George. The phone stood next to the three bottles of white wine that they had drunk to try and quench their thirst during the evening heatwave. Tiny droplets of water rolled off the last one. She could not sleep, and her thoughts had led her to an attempt to pinpoint how all of this had started.

People inherit a variety of things from their parents, whether good or bad. Evie now realised that the main things that she had taken on from her parents were their coping mechanisms for loneliness. This had begun when she moved away from home to study at university, as her joy at being independent quickly faded. She did not think that she really needed to act this way, but somehow, it seemed impossible not to. Whenever there was an opportunity to drink, she would never refuse and now that she was older, she drank whenever she came back home from work. Weekends were a haze of alcohol. Moreover, in between that, there were men. At the moment, there were only two. Ben was one of those who only came over for dinner and sex and rarely stayed the night. Simultaneously, she was dating George, but only after a few dates, she could already tell that he did not want anything serious, and she just had to accept that. Yet, at the same time, she was still in love with Aidan, who was such a vibrant person that his optimism had become contagious and so for once in her life, Evie had felt like everything was actually not as bad as it sometimes seemed to be. He had also been the only one who had taken away that feeling of loneliness, but Evie had soon realised that, just as her mother had told her, her love for him had ruined it and that he only wanted moments while Evie wanted eternity. This was the sort of love that could not last, but it was bound to linger.

He was also the only one who constantly showered her with compliments. When she was little, Evie couldn't understand what her mother needed from the men she spent time with because it was clear that she hardly liked any of them. Yet over the years, as she started to follow the same pattern, it dawned on her that her mother had been seeking praise and admiration, which was something that her father had never provided. Evie remembered how often she had heard every single one of her lovers call her beautiful and amazing. As overwhelming and empty as it may have been, this flattery filled a void in her that was there from that moment when her mother realised that someone she loved with all her heart had betrayed her and did not even appreciate her. However, Evie was certain that her father had loved her mother and had thought the same things, but had just never said them out loud because he assumed that she already knew how incredible she was.

She remembered thinking as a child that she would never drink, seeing what it had done to her father back then. Yet somehow, alcohol also held a positive quality in her mind since she had only ever seen her father's personality in those moments of intoxication. Therefore, she thought that maybe she could also find some sort of truth at the bottom of the many glasses of wine that she drank. Evie also remembered dreaming about finding her soulmate and knowing that she would only ever be with one man because, unlike her mother, she believed in true love. Yet here she was. A human being just as broken as the generation before her, if not more so.

Both of her parents were happy now, living their own lives and had moved on from their unhealthy habits. Her mother was with someone who was kind to her, and her father had remarried and now had another family to care for. Although Evie spoke to both of them frequently, they were always trivial conversations so that she still felt lost and alone. This loneliness was clawing away at her sanity and she wanted reassurance from them that she too would one day be normal. However, no matter how bad things would get, Evie knew that she would never talk to either of them about this because that was the way that things had always been unless Evie reached another breaking point and by then it might already be too late.

The Attic of My Mind

She still saw his smile in her mind. The way he looked under the fluorescent lights of their local fish and chips shop. They were drunk out of their minds. The paper's grease made their hands oily, but they were both so glad to have food that they did not mind. The two of them sat at the wonky metal table and, instead of talking, she just gave Henry an understanding smile every now and again as they chowed down on their six a.m. breakfast. That was the last time that she remembered feeling truly happy.

They parted at the train station, each going to a different side of town. She refused to accept what he had just said. As Henry turned to walk away, she held her hand against his cheek as if to say, 'don't make me let go'. She didn't want tomorrow to come because she couldn't cope with the thought of missing him. Yet as she saw him wave at her from a distance, she knew that it was time for her to make her way home too. Her steps echoed in the darkness, the crunch of the autumn leaves below her feet. That and her quiet sniffling brought on by her tears and the sound of her long trench coat swooshing against her legs was all that kept her company at this time of the morning. Along the way, she saw a couple of broken umbrellas that had been stolen by the windy city. She turned the usual corner to walk down one of the familiar streets; however, a huge barricade of 'no pedestrians' signs stretched before her as she did. Although she was mad at the fact that this city had once again inconvenienced her by surprise, she had no one to express her anger to, so she simply turned around and headed in the direction of the next side street.

Upon turning that corner, she was puzzled because the street led into a tunnel, seemingly connecting this street and the next. Perhaps it was the late hour or the number of drinks she had had, but she was quite sure that the tunnel hadn't been there whenever she had taken this way home before. It seemed to stretch ahead of her for quite a distance. As she walked through it, the eerie stillness and its pale green tiles made her feel uneasy. Something seemed wrong, and yet she could not pinpoint what was bothering her. Turning to look back at where she had come from, she was terrified to see that the tunnel entrance was no longer there. Panic overtook her and she started rushing forward into the unknown. Several smaller pathways appeared on the sides. Not seeing an end to it, she turned into one of them, getting completely lost. Her heart raced, her eyes had no more time for tears, and she felt pain shoot up and down her body from the strain of running. She turned corner after corner, and hallucinations seemed to crowd her as she started seeing scenes akin to something from a horror movie the deeper she wandered into the labyrinth that she found herself in – a woman getting lobotomised or a man beating a woman to death in one corner, her blood staining the mint coloured walls. Her mind went blank.

*

She was running down the tunnel.

The light had been so blinding that she hadn't noticed the cliff's edge that she fell onto and was now stranded on, with no way back up. Her side ached, and she knew that with her extremely sensitive skin would have bruises all over the next day. Did she have sensitive skin? She wasn't so sure any more. The more pressing question was how she would get off of this edge. The city stretched in the distance, enveloped by the cobalt tones of the evening. After checking her pockets and realising that she did not have her phone on her, she understood that her situation was particularly dire. She rested her back against the dusty rock of the cliff and closed her eyes, hoping for the best. Everything felt so familiar as if she had already been in this situation before. Neither the location nor the to-be bruises terrified her since she felt like this was something that she had dealt with in the past. Just at that moment, she heard someone whisper above her, 'Cleo.' A pause. 'Aphrodite, give me your hand.'

The voice, the names sent a wave of nostalgia over her, creating goosebumps all over her body. She decided to let this dream take her further.

'I'm here.'

'Can you reach up?'

She got up and raised her hand, feeling someone pull her up. The man before her looked friendly. He had slightly ginger hair and large glasses, just like the ones she used to wear when she was younger. Something about him seemed so familiar, so similar to someone from her past. His hand still held hers, although she was now safe.

'I need to get you back,' he said, true compassion marking his features. 'He is really worried about you this time. Did you hurt yourself? Last time you just climbed down there.'

'Who are you? What's happened?'

'Oh,' he took a step back, and compassion quickly turned to anxiousness. 'Last time you remembered.'

'Remembered what?' Suddenly, everything came rushing back to her. The tunnel, the first time she'd stepped into it, the man whose face she had seen as she opened her eyes, sitting in an upholstered armchair across from her, quietly inquisitive. The man had introduced himself as Dr H, or perhaps that was just how she remembered him. She remembered all the times that he had tried to tell her who she was. The endless hours of her sitting in his study as he repeated the phrase, 'You just need a bit more therapy, and then you'll finally understand. The real you is in there somewhere; you just need to let her out.'

He was so certain that he could fix her. He had tried to keep her busy, telling her that happiness can easily be achieved by keeping one's mind occupied and, therefore, away from negative thoughts. To achieve this, Dr H prepared a to-do list, and when she struck one thing off that list, another appeared in its place. The last task which she remembered doing before she attempted to escape yet again was pumpkin carving. He said it would be a good exercise, an attempt at catharsis. Yet, as she had scooped and prodded at the mushy insides of the bright and shiny pumpkin, she had only felt the rage build up inside her rather than disappear.

Alcohol was forbidden. According to him, that only unleashed the sad version of her, the version he wanted to eradicate. It just made her think too much. However, he had told her that if she felt the need to reflect on things, she should not keep it all inside her but rather share her thoughts and feelings with him. Therefore, she would often write essays where she delved into her thoughts and memories of the time before, which he would then read. One of them was called 'The Attic,' and she remembered sitting next to him as he read it. It made him cry, and he had told her that reading it made him feel like he was being nailed to a cross. All of this now bubbled up to the surface of her mind. Not only that. She now also remembered her previous escape attempts.

'I need to get you back. He'll be less upset this time if you don't remember,' the nice man suddenly stopped her train of thought.

At that moment, she wanted to scream at him that she did remember, but she hid that angst deep and instead pretended as though she was oblivious to what was happening.

The man escorted her through the tunnel, confident that he knew exactly where he was going, and they soon arrived at an exit that was impossible to see to the naked eye, perfectly concealed in a seemingly unremarkable stretch of the corridor. Beyond the door, she stopped paying attention to her surroundings because she had seen all of it before; the mansion with its countless rooms, the paintings, the fireplaces, the vibrant Persian carpets swallowing the floors. She could even lead the man to her room if she wanted to, but she preferred to maintain her act of complete ignorance.

As they passed through the living room, she saw the commotion outside on the terrace. There was a party going on with Dr H apparently in the position of both the host and the guest of honour as several people were huddled around him, patting him on the back and laughing at all of his jokes. However, she knew that his jokes were probably entirely nonsensical, he didn't have a great sense of humour. Even though his back was turned towards her, she noticed his slightly greying hair, and as he slowly started to turn around, she recognised his features. She remembered them from the fish and chips shop – that last moment of true happiness. Yet, how could it be him? She started to question her own mind again. The nice man watched the scene as intensely as she did, so she saw this as her opportunity. It took her seconds to get to the door and pull it open to run into the garden.

'He's kidnapped me, help me please!' she screamed, turning the once lively garden into a game of statues, as stillness had paralysed everyone.

Even though only a few minutes had passed since her dramatic entrance, it felt like hours as she closely scanned every face, searching for an ounce of empathy. Dr H finally stopped looking at her in a way which she could only describe as ominous before turning to the crowd and proclaiming;

'She is one of my patients. Please, everyone, meet Aphrodite. We have only been working together for a while, so she's still not feeling quite like herself.'

'I do feel like myself,' she said with as much conviction as she could muster, feeling tears sting her eyes.

'Owen, could you please take Aphrodite to her room?' Dr H asked the nice man in a way that mastered the art of being passive-aggressive so that she was genuinely impressed. Something about him saying her name made her realise that this name was not even hers.

'No. I can prove that you kidnapped me. My real name is Cleo Aston. I'm sure any of you could find me online; just try, please try. Someone, please try,' her pleading appeared to have worked as some people took out their phones.

'Owen, could you please give me her passport?' Dr H asked with a slightly patronising tone. He paused and then added, 'We take these away from our guests since their families are often worried about them leaving before they truly feel like themselves.' As he flashed it before her, she could see her picture there or at least the way she remembered herself alongside the name Aphrodite. He passed it to one of the guests, who inspected it, then passed it around.

'Are you kidding me? What is the passport going to say

about me? It's fake. You've faked it! There is nothing in there about who I actually am. What I like, what I am like, what I feel. The person you're showing me could be anyone.'

This was too overwhelming for Cleo. From the scene itself to the memories which kept twisting and turning inside her mind, making her unsure of who she saw before her. She remembered the first time that she had seen Dr H and he had not recognised her, but to her, he had looked so similar to Henry, from the intensity in his eyes right down to the tattoo peeking out beneath the sleeve of his shirt. It was him, she was sure of it, yet why was he doing it? Why was he trying to change her? Why was he trying to convince her that everything she felt was wrong and that the world she built inside her mind, that perfect image of happy love, was harmful and incorrect?

'I found her!' A man stepped forward. He was holding his phone in his hand and staring at Dr H with resentment and fear, 'She is who she says she is.' His arm slipped around Cleo's shoulders as more people started to take unsure steps away from Dr H.

'You don't know what you're doing. I was just trying to help her,' Dr H spoke, entirely unfazed by their reaction.

'Let's get you out of here.' The man and the two women who were with him at the party were leading Cleo towards the door, but she couldn't stop looking back. She did not want to let go, despite everything that had happened.

The streets looked exactly as they had the last time that she saw them. Cleo got into a car with her saviours, but when they asked her where they should take her, where her home was, she could not tell them because she no longer knew. In her mind, her home was now with Dr H, so instead they took her to their apartment.

*

Drops of rain started to fall just as they stepped outside the door of the building, pouring over the piles of leaves. It felt as though months had passed since those terrible events, and yet every morning, when Cleo opened the curtains of her bedroom window, the street below looked the same, not a single autumn leaf out of place. She was starting to feel more like herself every single day. The little things helped. James, the man who had saved her, was doing everything he could to try to help her remember who she used to be. These attempts consisted of him trying to find her favourite songs and let her listen to them on repeat to call back joyful memories or by taking her to a bar or café that she might have frequented. This helped immensely, as Cleo had always been great at preserving the past in her mind, so more and more things came back to her. Unfortunately, many of those memories were associated with Dr H or who she knew him as before, Henry. Staring at herself in the mirror was still difficult because, although she recognised herself, she hated the person who stood before her. How can you not when someone has tried to convince you that you should hate everything about yourself?

'Are you sure you're up for this?' James asked, a look of true concern complementing the kindness in his face.

'Yes, I can't let him get away with this.'

It was the first day of the hearing, as James had helped Cleo find a lawyer to take Dr H to court to charge him with kidnapping. Although feelings of love still lingered in her, she knew that what he had done was wrong and that she couldn't let it go unpunished. Courage was one of those forgotten feelings, but as she walked alongside James down the court building's dimly-lit corridor, it began to approach her as an old friend would.

'Here, have some of this,' James pulled out a piece of apple pie wrapped in a napkin. 'You need some comfort food.'

Cleo devoured the pie and once again felt grateful for the kindness of people.

They entered the hearing room where Dr H was already sitting at one of the tables. As Cleo turned to face the judges, she froze. Three women were sitting on the pedestal, each wearing a different colour yukata, their faces graced with geisha makeup. Their painted on diplomatic smiles were directed at Cleo. James looked just as puzzled as her, and so he went to speak to them. However, it quickly became clear that they could only speak Japanese.

'Do you want me to interpret for you?' Dr H asked, not a hint of smugness or sarcasm in his voice.

At that moment, Cleo realised that he had somehow arranged for this to be their panel of judges so that she wouldn't have a chance to defend herself, that she would never have this chance because he would not let her since he would never accept blame for what had happened. No amount of apple pie could help with that. Cleo pulled James aside and told him that they needed to leave and that this was not worth pursuing.

Incredulous at her words, James asked, 'But why would you let him get off scot-free?'

'Because I know that he won't bother me ever again. He wanted me to change, and I didn't, so he's given up now. I need to let go.'

The words stung as they left her mouth. From the moment that she entered the room, her eyes had kept looking towards him, but that look had not been returned. The iciness in his face showed how little he cared. Cleo could not process that apathy, and so without gracing him with another glance, she left the room.

James opened the door of his car, waiting for her to get in.

'I'll walk home. I remembered where my apartment is,' she gave him a hug with which she tried to convey all of the gratitude that she felt for his help.

'I'm worried. I don't want to just leave you like this. Will you be all right?'

'Don't worry, I'll be me.'

The rain had stopped. The hour was early, and people were only just starting to leave their houses to go to work. Cleo turned the usual corner to walk down one of the familiar streets. It was clear of 'no pedestrians' signs.

*

'The Attic: an essay.

When Margaret Thatcher was Prime Minister, she requested an architect to reconstruct Downing Street's interior to match what it would have looked like during the eighteenth century and when that was done, she lived in the attic, above the perfectly restored history. A miserably accurate metaphor. Can this not be applied to me, living in my own little isolated world, while I try to preserve an immaculate version of the past that I have constructed but which no longer has any connection to reality? I catch myself remembering only what I want to remember.

It is nice to be cared for, but it's sometimes nicer to care, and I did for him. Not the way he said he did, using those words as a weapon against me. Trying to make me change, constantly reprimanding me for not letting him in. Implying that I wasn't giving enough, that I was never enough, would never be enough. The fact that he left me without even giving me a chance to show him that we could work breaks my heart. Now I feel certain that hiding my heart and then being rejected still leaves room for some hope that it wasn't because of me, my personality, me rushing things, but showing my heart and being rejected, precisely due to who I am, is bound to make me go insane. Especially if I've given them the whole of me because that hurts more than these words can describe since I have only ever given pieces of myself to people because of the fear that the entire me was not worthy of love. Softly, life put its hands over my eyes and turned me into a vacuum of my own thoughts, what I wished to see. Nobody should have to beg for love, but I feel like I constantly did.

    I do feel plainer and saner now, but these feelings are still here. The feelings that taste like cookie dough, comforting but tainted with guilt, because I feel like a burden, because I still love him, but I feel like he's waiting for me to change, and I just can't. He's like my favourite drink. I need a refill all the time. The moments we shared were never in technicolour, rather black and white, covered with a hazy indigo filter, marked by beautiful serenity and sadness. I wish I could turn him back into a stranger so it would be easier to say goodbye. If you're reading this now, I wish I was see-through, and I wish that you wouldn't hold it against me that I'm not.'

Holding back the Years

Beatrice thought that the last thing on his mind was to leave her, but she could not have been more wrong. Not only had he done it, but he had ended things in such a way that rendered everything they had shared over the last seven years meaningless. She sat beside the windows inside a café, watching the passers-by through the slight fog that had built up over the glass. Steam rose from her coffee cup as she sank deeper into her seat and let her mind go through everything that had happened. Now every time she closed her eyes, she remembered how Oliver used to hold her in his arms as they lay beneath the sheets of their first freezing apartment and say, 'Birdie, promise me that this will always be us.'

At the time, she believed that he meant that they should stay together and, more importantly, stay in love but now, after everything that had happened, she realised that he had actually meant that they should never grow old.

His attachment to the past had been one of the things that had made her fall in love with him, as he would always cherish every single one of their memories together, remembering it in the utmost detail. But what was magical at first soon became difficult since he was rarely even present in those moments but rather remembered them longingly afterward.

His favourite quirk had been reading the little plaques placed on benches, which marked the moments people had spent there together. The two of them were once walking along a seafront, and as they sat down to watch the sunset, Oliver read the note out loud, 'In loving memory of Ellie who loved watching the swans as much as I loved seeing her smile, George.'

Beatrice thought that reading this had nearly brought him to tears. He had said that they should leave such a note somewhere to mark a particularly wonderful moment. Yet, as with all his quirks, this one soon began to worry her because he started suggesting that they leave such testimonials everywhere so that the whole town would be full of their memories. She had laughed at the idea but then realised that he was serious. Eventually, they started doing just that, and now that their relationship was over, Beatrice knew that nearly everywhere she went, she would be reminded of their moments together, painful reminders scattered everywhere.

When their relationship took a turn for the worse, and there were many more negative memories to look back on, it struck Beatrice that he would never remember the events as they were. Rather he would put his own spin on them, more often than not, trying to minimise the argument they had just had or trying to portray himself as the innocent party, which became increasingly problematic because when you have to start arguing with a memory instead of the person before you, it is no longer a fair fight. Yet, he had told Beatrice when they first met that he could only appreciate emotions when looking back at the past, and although it had worked for him for most of his life, it had begun to take its toll on their relationship and, even more than that, his mind, not long ago.

At the beginning of their time together, they often went on day trips to small towns and walked around until late in the evening. They had so much to talk about that it felt as though someone had sped up time. At night, Oliver was always busy with events and parties, and he took her with him. It was a whirlwind of late nights, dancing until you could no longer move, immense quantities of alcohol, drugs and people who you saw only once. Oliver loved being among people and needed these evenings out. However, he didn't necessarily like the people he met at these events. Rather, he liked to talk to them only so that he could 'figure them out'. Beatrice loved that he did that since he could then let her in on his thoughts about them. The only thing he never did was tell her what he thought of himself, so she had to dissect his personality on her own.

 Beyond his attachment to the past, Oliver was also very creative. This seemed unusual for someone who studied law, which is how they had met, as they were doing the same degree, so she was glad that she had found someone like him. When it came to his artistic skills, he had a lot of talent. He could draw and paint just about anything, but he preferred abstract paintings. Beatrice was often awoken by him painting in the middle of the night. A huge canvas covered in dark colours with shapes that sometimes scared her, resembling the ghouls from her childhood nightmares. At one point, however, he found a new hobby. Because he didn't have a lot of money, he started going to charity shops to buy bad paintings since he could just pull them off the frame and use the frame as his own after stretching some material over it. But what used to be a practical endeavour turned into something else when he decided that he would buy unremarkable landscapes and paint one cartoon character or another on them and then sell them on. That was the peak of his business because a surprising amount of people bought his embellished landscapes whether they had Courage the Cowardly Dog or Tom from Tom & Jerry on them. Beatrice knew that this was childish, but she didn't mind, because it never impacted her life negatively.

However, sometimes, when she was looking at him paint yet another character onto yet another painting, she couldn't help but feel like he should try to aspire to greater things.

Beyond that, this creativity manifested itself not only through his paintings but also in how he spoke. Every time they met, he kissed her and then would tell her a new story that he had just heard.

Once they had met in a park before going on a walk, and he had immediately said, 'Did you know that in Argentina, if a dog attacks you, then you can't defend yourself, for example, by throwing stones at it, but the only thing you can do is bark at it? That's according to the law.'

Or yet another time; 'In Japan, if a husband forgets his wife's birthday, she is allowed to kill him, as long as she does so with her bare hands. That's just crazy, right?'

It seemed as though he read a page from a *Fact of the Day* Calendar while she was not at home, but he didn't. He just found out about these things somehow. She knew that life with him would never be boring.

She remembered the first time that they went out for a drink. These stories were what drew her in. It was as though he was hypnotising her by giving her so much to constantly laugh about. In the first ten minutes, he had told her that he was a painter and was very interested in witch trials at that moment. This led to a long conversation about everything that he had discovered during his research for his paintings. After spending hours talking in a bar, they had gone back to her place and, in the middle of one of his stories, he put his arms around her and told her that she was his favourite new thing to figure out, precisely because he couldn't fully understand her. Moments later, Beatrice refused to give him a hug because she was too absorbed in smoking her cigarette and swaying to the music that she had put on, and she added, 'Suffering is part of human existence.' Oliver gave her the biggest smile she had ever seen before bursting out in laughter.

'I feel like I'm about to start dating myself.'

But first impressions do not charm for too long. The beginning of their relationship was like something out of her favourite books, but now she knew that it was time to put her heart back on the shelf.

Their first real fight was the only one that still made sense to Beatrice because the reasons for their fights just became more and more irrational as time went on. When they had both already graduated and began working as trainees, Oliver had come home one day and announced that he would no longer continue his traineeship. He had lasted at the firm for only three months. Still, when Beatrice asked him what had made him quit, he replied with a shrug and said that he despised the routine of it, the nine to five predictability, the fact that he was always tired and so could not find the energy to do anything creative but, most of all, he despised the fact that it made him feel like a grown-up. Following that, he chose to only work in bars. Because he still earned money from it but could stay close to the night scene and always had to stay until late at night, which meant that he could paint during the day. Beatrice often mentioned other opportunities to him, but she soon realised that she would have to surrender when it came to this topic the day that Oliver told her that in addition to working in bars at night, he would also work as a Segway tour guide during the day because he loved the idea of being on the move. It was impossible to reason with him; therefore, even though this argument had been a recurring one, it died down after a while.

The fight that followed was what would eventually lead to

the bitter end of their relationship. One day Oliver had rushed into the flat, his cheeks rosy from excitement and had told her that he had something to show her. He took her hand and led her to the car park only a few steps away from their flat. Oliver pointed to a worn-down school bus and proudly announced that he had bought it for practically nothing at an auction and that he planned to restore it and turn it into an RV. Beatrice did not know what to say as she slowly walked around the bus, but the only thing that came to mind was that there is nothing more ironic and appropriate than the idea of a person who is afraid to grow old deciding to buy a school bus and living in it.

The last few months of their relationship were unbearable for Beatrice, who saw the love of her life slowly slipping away. Once they started fighting all the time about the RV, he had seen it as a sign that their relationship was over when Beatrice never thought it was. He began to see other people. The problem was that he never told her. Like a child, he was afraid of his secret for fear of being scolded if he would tell her, so she found out about this by accident. One night, when she was looking out of her window, desperate for him to come home, she saw a girl go into his bus. Nothing more was needed. She confronted him, but he told her that this girl was slightly crazy, as most creative people are, so he had ended things with her anyway so she had nothing to worry about. All he had to do for her to forgive him was look into her eyes and say all of the cliché things that had already been said before;

'Sorry for being such a mess. I'm sorry that I hurt you. I care for you so much and I am just hopeless at expressing it.'

It took everything she had to be stern with him because she didn't know how to be angry at him.

'You have to do better from now on, Oliver. I don't want

you to hurt me again, and I don't want you to mess with my mind again.'

'I won't. I promise. I just felt a bit lost in life, so I acted out instead of talking to you about it. I'm sorry.'

Beatrice held his head in her hands as he pressed it against her chest. Oliver really did not know how to express his emotions for someone who was so great at talking. He knew how to talk about them abstractly, as he did with memories, but nothing he ever said felt truly real or heartfelt. There was a distance between them, and it had always been there because of his ways, so Beatrice knew that even though she had forgiven him, he wouldn't change and that it would only be a matter of time before they found themselves in this place again.

Oliver pulled her onto the shabby bed and started placing kisses all over her body. She closed her eyes and drifted off into familiar feelings.

'I missed this,' Oliver said, reaching for a can of beer across her body. She slowly ran her fingertips across the freckles on his chest. Music was playing from his phone in the background as Oliver sang along to a Hall & Oates song:

You're out of touch, I'm out of time, but I'm out of my head when you're not around.

He had told her that he associated every song with a specific memory, and so once, she had made him put on one of his playlists and tell her what memory went with each song. He had avoided telling her anything about this one. As much as she loved hearing him sing those words, she didn't think that they were meant for her.

When she was leaving the next morning, Oliver stopped her by the door and said, 'Thanks for putting up with me.' He held her hands.

Beatrice placed a kiss on his cheek and gave him a smile.

Oh, it's not that difficult when you really want to, she thought to herself as she was walking away from the bus.

*

They started seeing each other more frequently again, with Beatrice even spending time with him in the bus that she loathed so much. But then, only a month later, when Beatrice had already become used to seeing him again and them having shared the same sweetness as they had in the early days of their relationship, that was to come to an end. They were to have dinner together one night, so she made her way to the bus with a couple of boxes of Italian takeaway, and as he opened the door, she could already tell that something was wrong.

'How was your day?' Beatrice attempted to make conversation while putting the food on paper plates, but Oliver didn't say anything besides 'Good' before lying down on the bed.

'Are you okay?' She tried again, handing him a glass of wine.

'Yes, I'm fine. I just want to be alone tonight.'

'Oh, okay. Well, we can just have dinner, and then I could go,' she said, trying to ignore the pang she felt in her chest.

'I'm not hungry.'

'Oliver, what's wrong?'

'Nothing. I just feel like I want to do some painting tonight.'

Beatrice sat down beside him on the bed and kissed him.

'I understand.' Her hand passed over his slightly greying hair.

'Come here,' Oliver pulled her onto his lap and placed his forehead against hers before giving her a kiss. 'Have a good night.'

Beatrice stood up to leave.

'Oliver, before I go, will you tell me a story?'

'I suppose I can spare a moment before getting to the art.' He smiled. He was quiet for a while, clearly rifling through the many stories that filled his mind.

Finally, he spoke, 'So my mother and father had been together for twenty years when this happened. I was there with them, which was a rare occasion. They went to the store one Saturday to buy groceries. They get to the store and start going through the aisles. They get to the fruit section, and my mother picks up a box of strawberries. And as she does this, my father says to her: "Listen, Joanie, don't get these big strawberries, they are not as sweet, get the smaller ones". The next thing I know, my mother is throwing this box of strawberries at him and yelling. Apparently, he had said the same thing to her nearly every time they went to the store for twenty years, and every single time she had patiently explained that she prefers the big ones, and since he doesn't even eat the strawberries, it's not really up to him. Yet he just never listened. This had manifested in other areas of their lives as well. So it turns out that even after twenty years, he had no idea what she liked. They split up after that but got back together soon afterward. I just remembered tonight that I keep forgetting to ask my mother whether he still says anything about the strawberries.'

Beatrice felt a lump in her throat as she closed the door behind her. She couldn't sleep that night, so when she heard the first sounds of the morning flutter and fuss at five o'clock, she got up and went to the window. Oliver's bus wasn't there. The empty space in the parking lot tore her apart, and she wished she could see that damn bus there again. She tried to contact him, but he would not reply, and Beatrice realised that she would probably never see him again. He had disappeared and, whatever life he would now lead, he did not want her to be a part of it.

Beatrice was fully aware that she had flaws. Two of which stood out more than most. She knew that she could easily become obsessed, whether with things, art, or people. Although this was troubling, it was really the latter that caused some difficulties. Since becoming obsessed with people was generally frowned upon but, more than that, once she had shown her heart to someone and they no longer found her to be a mystery, this used to turn into rejection. Beatrice had lost count of how many times rejection had scarred her because she had chosen the wrong people and had preferred to see them as the image that she held in her mind rather than what they were truly like. However, she had never been able to understand that until it was too late.

Her second flaw was directly linked to the former since she had the constant need to control everything and everyone. This is why her relationship with Oliver was so complicated since she couldn't control him because one can't control those in control and, no matter how chaotic Oliver appeared, he constantly knew what he was doing. More than that, what really irked Beatrice was that she was constantly so introspective, so focused on analysing herself, while Oliver never gave it a second thought when it came to his own character. And yet he knew exactly who he was, being so sure of himself. More than that, what Beatrice realised when looking back at their time together was that Oliver probably had a better understanding of who she was than she did. He had figured her out and so was no longer interested in her, moving on to his next favourite new thing. While at the same time, her image of Oliver may not have been accurate at all.

The irony of delving into her memories of their time together was not lost on her, so Beatrice finished the last of her now already cold coffee and decided to stop reflecting on this. She had to go through these memories in her mind because she was too afraid of once again becoming susceptible to living a life she couldn't leave behind, afraid of carrying this pain and hurt in her heart. And now that she had, she knew that he too would soon become a memory, left in the past where he belongs.

Bed of Regrets

The cold was unbearable. The kind of cold that works its way through your bones, shaking every little cell in your body. The heater turned on, under her blanket, Anna still felt it. It was her loneliness that was creeping its way through her. She needed someone next to her, someone to hold her, to take away this feeling.

This time she was on a beach. A vast beach with cliffs covered in moss and grass. Maybe a crumbling castle on the shore. Somewhere truly picturesque. She would be wrapped up in her layers; a beautiful burgundy coat and thick wool scarf, holding a camera in her gloved hands, taking shots of the scenery. Someone by her side. She would feel happy and excited about going to get a hot chocolate afterwards. They would sit outside at a wonky table and watch the colourful leaves fall to the ground. It would have been a day out, an adventure. When people at work asked her what she was up to that weekend, she would tell them about it.

Anna awoke at four in the morning, as usual. There was a stillness in the air that she was already familiar with. She took a shower, still shivering. The warm water barely touched her soul. She put on her makeup and her work clothes, made her coffee and headed out. There was hardly anyone on the streets, she had the bus to herself and when she finally reached the office building, except for the guards, there was no one else there. She spent the first half hour at her desk sipping her coffee and looking at the grey fog outside the window, hugging the city below with its sleepy blanket.

At around eight thirty people started appearing. They were all tired and groggy and barely paid any attention to her; she was just a fixture in the office. She turned to her work, knowing that all of her productivity would be gone by lunchtime anyway. At eleven o'clock, she went for her coffee break with Austin and Olivia. They asked her what she had done over the weekend and she merely said that she had had a calm weekend, just like always, just the way she liked it. Austin brought up the open mic bar again, the one she had said nothing about last time he mentioned it. Olivia said they should all go there on Friday. This time Anna said she had other plans so she would not be able to make it.

The day was just like any other day. The monotonous sounds of typing. The voices sharing pleasantries. Anna was imagining the bar. The dark little alcoves, the faint smell of alcohol that has seeped into the floor, the cute tables, the warmth radiating from people, the musicians bringing life to the stage. She would dream of it, she knew.

When she got home, she put on her cosy pyjamas and microwaved her leftover pasta. Anna settled on the sofa and turned on the Netflix true crime series she had just started. When she finished dinner, she took a piece of paper and wrote down: 'Open mic bar with Austin and Olivia on a Friday night' and she took it to her bedroom, where she placed it in the box stowed underneath her bed. The box was filling up; she had already had to purchase a bigger one. Innocently, she had thought that when she first started it, seeing it pile up, seeing all those missed opportunities it would shake her out of it. It would overwhelm her with guilt and regret, and a terrible kind of sadness that would make her change her ways. Even though she could not remember exactly how long ago she had started it, she knew it had been too long now. Nothing seemed to help.

It had come from something her therapist had said, back when she had attempted to fix her issues. She had suggested that Anna try to visualise the mountain of experiences and adventures she had turned down because she was too scared to accept them. Anna had also abandoned the idea of a therapist long ago, but she had liked this concept. However, clearly it had been a failure.

She recalled when she first started collecting these invitations. Back then she had a different job and two best friends, although they both lived quite far away. The very first one she wrote down was an invitation from her friend Josie, to come and stay with her for a few days in Dublin. She had said no because the idea of the trip filled her with anxiety and she couldn't really understand why. It wasn't the first time she had been invited over, it was more so that she needed to write it down because it had become ridiculous how many times she had found excuses as to why she couldn't go. Anna thought maybe it would serve as a reminder that she needs to finally do this. However, she just couldn't find the strength within herself to book tickets and plan a trip. So she just let the idea sit at the back of her mind and she could feel Josie grow more distant, week by week, until finally Josie was no longer the one to reach out first and Anna felt too awkward to do it herself. That's how she lost Josie. A friend she had had since she was a teenager.

Almost the same happened with Melanie. Another friend she had been able to keep close to her for years, ever since they were in primary school. Melanie kept inviting her to festivals and concerts, or really any other type of event. She was the outgoing type, the kind to never sit still, which is why it's even a miracle that her and Anna were friends. So when Anna kept declining her offers, Melanie just seemed to slowly forget about her. The invitations became more and more sparse until, finally, they just stopped, leaving Anna on the verge of a nervous breakdown having realised that her inability to go out and socialise had left her without any real friends.

This inability to do things was not brought on by something extraordinary. Anna could not even blame it on some horrible thing that happened to her that made her not want to be part of the world any more. That's the thing, she did want it, but not the reality of it. She wanted it her way, the way she made up those scenarios in her mind. It had started gradually and increased with time. Saying no here and there, to saying no to everything.

But she didn't want to think about this now. Anna lay down in her bed, trying to push away all of these thoughts that kept reminding her how small her life had become. She wanted to be somewhere else. Not the bar with Austin and Olivia, as this would still be too painful. Some time would have to pass before she could dream of that scenario.

An abandoned church and a small cemetery beside it. Perhaps at dusk. When the last light of the day peeks through the trees. She would wander the paths along the graves, looking at the names. The couples buried together, the families. Juliet, Robert and much later their son Alfred. Together even in death. All of these different people together, in the same place, when it was so very likely that they hated each other, or merely disliked each other, had they met, when they were alive. Cemeteries inspire a sense of unity. This feeling that although every single one of us is on our own in life that ultimately we would come together. Anna liked the thought. She would enter the church. Sit down on one of the wooden pews, withered from age and barely holding her weight, and someone would sit next to her. A friend, a lover. They would enjoy that moment of silence. Because it would not be silence if they were together, their breathing filling the void in the empty hall.

No. She wants to feel the sun on her skin. They are in Italy. Sipping Aperol Spritzes after a long day of walking around. Her cameral roll is full of photos of statues and lovely little streets of cobblestones and buildings with vines growing on them. She needs these photos for the memories. To prove that she has been there. Then again, in her perfect world she wouldn't need to prove anything to anyone. They are somewhere in summertime. Her skin bronze and healthy. The evening full of possibilities.

*

The following day at work was slightly different. Austin appeared at her side long before their coffee break and, sitting on the edge of her desk, asked her if she was doing okay. Of course she was, she said, as always. Yet Anna could see the look he gave her, which meant that he did not believe her. Nevertheless, she could not unravel herself before him, could not put the burden on him. If he only knew how much she wanted to be his friend. A real friend, not just a colleague you go for a coffee break with. However, she knew how attached she would get, she felt like she would push him away the moment she started revealing herself to him. It would be too much for anyone to handle. It was already too much for her.

Then again, maybe it wouldn't. She entertained the thought for a second, but no, she couldn't do that to him. Moreover, to herself, because if he suddenly thought she was weird and would start to shy away from her, it would kill her. If he told Olivia

'Anna is strange, maybe we shouldn't invite her along for coffee any more,' she would not be able to handle it. She was interrupted by Austin, who was still at her desk and was now asking her if she would like to go for some Greek food later with him and Olivia. Although she hates Greek food, she wants to say yes, but she says she can't, she's so sorry. She already has dinner plans. Two invites in one week is not the norm and Anna feels as though he is pressuring her, as though he can see that something is not quite right.

Anna spent the rest of the day at work feeling extremely anxious as she wasn't sure how long she could keep up this façade and pretend that she actually had things to do. She was sure that at some point Austin and Olivia would start to take her rejection personally. There would be nowhere left for her to hide. When the work day was over and she made her way home, she stopped at her local store and stocked up on vodka and coke. She knew it would be one of those nights.

*

It was Christmas Eve but it felt more like Halloween. There was no snow on the ground, just bare trees all around and an eerie atmosphere as it seemed that no one was at home. Everyone was with their families, probably in their magnificent houses in the suburbs or abroad, not in an apartment building on the outskirts of the city. Anna sat in the dark and drank her cinnamon and apple tea while watching *Love Actually* for the umpteenth time. The sounds of joviality filled her ears and mind through her headphones and she could almost imagine herself there, among the characters, participating in all of these variations of Christmas. Her favourite storyline had always been the one with

Colin Firth. She wanted that love story and the ending, where he returns to France, to Aurélia, and everyone in the restaurant is excited for their love and cheers them on. It filled her heart with jealousy, the idea of having that many people around you and happy for you. The end credits of couples in the airport rolled and she could feel tears in her eyes but before she could truly embrace her sadness, she saw a dark figure in the doorway of her bedroom. Before she even realised what was happening, she felt a sharp pain on the side of her head and her mind went dark, still swimming with airport scenes.

She woke up with a horrible headache and struggled to open her eyes. She could tell her forehead and cheek were wet. Dark red stains covered her pyjama top. She could tell she was tied to her radiator. Her room was bright with light and there was a man rifling through her cupboards. He was tall and wearing a ski mask. It still took her a while to figure out what was happening.

'Fuck,' she heard him mutter. More like spit the words out. He had a point; she was not a good option for a robbery. There was hardly anything valuable in her house except her laptop and her phone. She didn't even wear jewellery, except for the one ring she always had on her ring finger which she had inherited from her mum.

She could see him turn around and so she closed her eyes. He moved towards the bed and she heard him bend down. He was pulling out the box from underneath her bed. Her eyes opened of their own volition. The box was on the bed and he was picking up the pieces of paper by the handful. Again, without being able to control herself, Anna started crying. She didn't care if he had looked inside her underwear drawer or seen her vibrator in the bedside table but the fact that he was seeing this, even though he most likely didn't even know what it meant to her, made her feel completely exposed and vulnerable.

Anna now realised that he was here, in her apartment, because of course he thought that she was not at home. Who has their lights turned off on Christmas Eve, except if they are not at home? Actually, come to think of it, she had had them turned off all day. The darkness had just felt more comforting. She lives on the ground floor and her blinds were open so he most likely broke in through one of the windows, and she hadn't heard him break it because she was watching that stupid film with her headphones on. He probably thought this would be an easy place to rob. Maybe she deserved to be robbed because of her carelessness. Yet now he was here with her. With his hands in the most valuable possession she had and even though he didn't understand its meaning, she felt as though he was judging her. She did think it was quite amusing that he looked there, because people did usually hide their valuables under their bed, didn't they? For her it was the life she could have had. Yet now he was merely digging through pieces of paper. It made her chuckle out loud.

This earned her another strike to the head. Anna did not even mind. The delirium was more pleasant than reality. She could feel herself drift away. The last thing that she thought of was that Austin had said that he was here over the Christmas holidays. That he had invited a couple of friends over because he couldn't afford to buy tickets back home since they were so expensive by the time he decided to buy them. Anna kept imagining what it would have been like to be at Austin's. She knew that if she had only mentioned that she would be alone, he would have invited her over.

She would have rung the doorbell in her red velvet dress that made her look like a Christmas gift herself. Austin would open the door with a radiant smile; the smile that had drawn her in when she first saw him. She would have a beautifully wrapped gift for the gift exchange later on and a bottle of wine for him. Austin would invite her in, to the warmth, to the smells of mulled wine and a roast dinner. He was good at hosting; she had heard this from others. She would talk to new people and laugh. They would maybe play a board game. Austin was a big fan of them. She would leave in the early hours of the morning, pleasantly tipsy from the mulled wine. She would ask Austin for the recipe and he would say that it was the standard recipe but that the secret ingredient was orange juice, a bit of orange zest and a touch of chili to give it a kick. She would make her way home on foot and as she passed the park in the middle of town, light snowflakes would start to fall. At first, she would think it was a trick of the light, maybe just rain. But no, it would be snow. A peach fuzz layer of snow quickly covering the ground and her hair. She would wrap herself up more tightly and rush home, still smiling about the evening. She would open her door and find a broken window, her place ransacked, her laptop missing. However, it wouldn't matter. She would call a company in the next few days to fix the window and she would replace her laptop. After all, it was not that expensive. And she would throw out the box. It wouldn't be necessary anymore because she would have had an adventure. A night to call a memory.

Act Naturally

The day begins with a carefully constructed routine. The routine is adapted to the interests and traits of the particular character in mind. Reginald has learnt to survive with only four hours of sleep each night, so the morning and day ahead is never challenging for him. After the night has been spent preparing for the coming day, he feels a great and immeasurable sense of satisfaction. This Saturday morning, however, he is still soundly asleep. The reason for this is his choice of character for the day, since this time it is Louis from the film *Interview with a Vampire*. Therefore, he has no reason to wake until night time when the sun can no longer hurt him.

Reginald no longer has an identity of his own. He is solely composed of the different characters he has portrayed to the world. He is not a great actor, and he has never claimed to be one, but he enjoys this game and the possibilities that arise for an ordinary individual when he discovers how many distinct personalities he can embody. It gives one a sense of limitless power and destroys the uniqueness that belongs to each of us but creates one of a different kind in its stead. His favourite event as a child had been Halloween, and so, through him believing that there was nothing remarkable about him, he had embraced his childhood passion as his everyday life so that now every day for him was Halloween as he constantly put on a new mask.

At seven o'clock, the sky had become a dark violet blanket, and so he awoke. He dressed in a respectable suit, painted his skin a paler colour and, after inspecting the newspaper for the showtimes of a film, he left his rather dreary abode. The streets were busy with Saturday crowds and, as he made his way through them, with the arrogance and cruel air of a nineteenth-century plantation owner who had unexpectedly become a creature of the night, his mask of pale skin and doleful eyes revealed that Louis had come to life. Saturday being a day of leisure ensured that his evening plan was already clear. He would go to a rather costly restaurant, order tempting and extravagant food but shun it after only slightly tasting it, because the creature he was imitating would have no interest in food. Then he would head to the cinema for a midnight showing of the film *Before Sunrise* because he wished to experience the longing for sunlight. He had planned to portray Louis in advance precisely because he knew that the film would be shown on this day and this was as close as he could get to imitating the scene from the film where Louis saw a sunrise for the first time in years.

The film inspired surprisingly deep emotions, and he found himself holding back tears. After everyone, including himself, had left the theatre, he remained outside of it for a moment, admiring the gothic building. Then he turned and left, leaving behind yet another aspect of his character of the day. He walked quickly, fearing someone was following him. Perhaps it was Lestat. Once he reached his door, he felt incredible ease overtake his dead heart.

*

Reginald wasn't entirely sure that being dead was the most tragic state one could find himself in, so the choice of character for the following Monday was Winston Smith, the oppressed and traumatised hero of George Orwell's *1984*. He was not a difficult person to impersonate, thought Reginald. All he had to do was cough a lot, smoke, barely eat and write extensive and intense diary entries about his day. He was fortunate enough to live in a society where, even though oppression by the government and ceaseless surveillance was ever so present, it was not as strict and publicly accepted as in the book.

    He had bought very drab and worn looking clothing from the local charity shop and was proud of his resemblance to his imagined portrait of Winston. Sitting by an open window where the breeze chilled him to the bone, he drank the cheapest coffee he could find and dedicated himself to writing down Winston's thoughts. Upon dusk, Reginald found himself in a small street, pressing one of the doorbells of a poorly constructed apartment building. The door opened, and he walked in. Coughing and breathing heavily, he climbed the stairs to the fourth floor and was greeted by an open door, in which stood a woman whose eyes were aglow with curiosity.

    'Don't make me guess. I always seem to make a fool of myself,' she said as she took his hand and quickly led him into the apartment. It was by no means a very pleasant place to reside in, but it served its purpose; there was a bed, located beside the window which was sealed with plastic tape at the edges to not let cold air in, a kitchen area where all cupboards looked used beyond their years, and the gas stove appeared to be an accident simply waiting to happen, and a main living area where there was a small cupboard and also a table, upon which Nina had placed a teapot and two assorted cups, as well as inexpensive biscuits. Despite the tragic state of all the items there, the overall impression was rather cosy and neat.

    Nina stood before him in her best attire. He knew this

because he had seen it many times before, and it was always taken out of the wardrobe, especially for him. It was a pencil skirt which used to be of a cream colour but with endless washings had turned slightly grey and a cherry silk blouse with a bow upon her chest. Her hair was of a gunmetal black colour, and her skin was pearly alabaster. This combination and her overly rouged cheeks were why Reginald had been attracted to her the first time he saw her in a café that he frequented and where she was working as a waitress. Nina's appearance reminded him of a childhood book he had, which was a very old illustrated edition of *Snow White*, where the drawings perfectly matched her looks.

From their first encounter onwards, Reginald became a regular at the café, surprising and amusing Nina with his daily transformations between characters. She told him that it brought excitement to her otherwise dull days because it seemed to be the only thing that could make her laugh or smile any more. Reginald grew even fonder of her because of these words. When she first asked him out for a drink, the only thing he could say was: 'Did somebody put you up to this?' But Nina had just laughed and not long after that they went out one evening to a restaurant that Reginald could afford and Nina would not feel uncomfortable in, and afterward they ended the night in Nina's apartment. That night Reginald saw no flaws in her dwellings.

'Think of a book. Communist society, rats, oppression.'

'I truly don't know, darling,' Nina poured the Tetley tea into the cup and motioned for Reginald to sit down on the side of the bed while she gracefully sat down upon the floor, placing her knees below her.

'1984. Winston Smith.'

'I've heard of the book but never read it.'

'It's about a man who lives in a totalitarian society where

material pleasures are unimaginable and everyone is forced to think the same. But he does meet a woman with who he falls in love, even though it's forbidden. And they meet in a secret apartment, small but cosy for the standards of that particular society. They manage to live a decadent life, delighting in the simplest things such as coffee and good food, and they make love passionately and without restrictions.'

'Now you're simply teasing me.'

Reginald joined her on the floor through a coughing fit and leaned in to place a kiss on her cheek, 'I promise you, I'm not.'

'You choose rather sad characters to be,' she said while stroking his face.

'Everything that is depressing has great appeal to me.' Nina nodded. Unknowingly, she had wandered into a subject that she did not want to discuss. Her hand had found his, and she squeezed it gently.

'Do you want to hear your horoscope for today?' She picked up the daily newspaper. 'Which one should I read – yours or your character's?'

Reginald smiled and gave her a kiss.

They made love that evening, and, once Nina was asleep, he dressed and left her studio, wandering into a nearby liquor store where he purchased a bottle of cheap gin. He had never stayed over because he did not want her to see him as he truly was and also how he prepares for his characters. At home, with a glass in his hand, he began to get ready for the following day. It would be Travis Bickle next. *Taxi Driver* had always held a special place in his heart, and he felt it was finally appropriate to attempt to imitate the insane Travis. He would have to improve on his accent, though. Reginald put the film on in the background while he thought about what he would wear. Finally, he chose jeans and a blue checked shirt. It was three in the morning when he had finished his preparation. Reginald took off his clothes, neatly folded them and put them back into the closet for future use, in case he would impersonate Winston again or they would probably be useful for some other character. He washed his face to remove the sickly make-up and then went into his bedroom.

    This was the only moment when Reginald was himself, stripped of all his attire, his mask, of the entire character. He held a profound distaste for the man, who seemed to be alive during the few minutes before slumber. He was incredibly plain and absolutely tedious. Reginald did not remember when he had first sensed this extreme hatred for himself. Perhaps it had always been within him, and the moment when he had first embodied someone else, he had been acting against this hatred for the first time. The very first character Reginald became was Bruce Wayne. It had been a pre-meditated choice because Bruce's secret identity made Reginald feel unique and, in a certain manner, superior to everyone else. At no point during those three days, since at first he used to embody characters for a longer period of time, did he become Batman, but just the thought that his alter-ego had an alter-ego was very amusing to him.

*

The alarm clock rang with a screeching sound, and Reginald leapt up in bed. He had been so consumed by his nightly thoughts that he had fallen asleep without the covers drawn upon his shivering body. The apartment was still. Time always seemed to stop when he was alone and without his façade of an exaggerated character. Coffee was quickly made, cereal was eaten, and then Reginald dressed and set off into the terrifying world. He worked in the back of a department store where a uniform was not a requirement, so he was at liberty to express himself. However, Reginald knew that he had to set certain limits, so on work days, he chose characters who were more subtle and left the flamboyant ones for the weekend. The people he worked with were used to his ways by now and also co-workers came and went, but he had worked at the store for six years now so no one dared reprimand him, nor did they laugh at his peculiar nature out of quiet respect. His days were always uneventful and always the same, so his odd habit was somewhat of a blessing since it ensured that at least he changed throughout the days.

Yet by the end of this day, Reginald was indescribably weary of embodying Travis because even though the film had been so eventful and daring, he knew that his impersonation of Travis faded in comparison because he was not willing to kill anybody or rescue a child prostitute from the miserable lifestyle that she was forced to live. After work, he once again headed to Nina's studio to seek comfort in her enthusiasm of him being yet another character she did not know.

Though Nina awaited him in her synthetic silky robe with her hair curled unevenly, looking as appealing as ever, Reginald did not delight in her company that evening because he didn't enjoy his own. This impersonation had been a failure, and he was aware of it, for the aim of his game was to make him like himself, but instead, he had achieved the goal of impersonating someone not unlike himself. Reginald concluded that he would have to raise the level of eccentricity for his character ever so slightly so that he would cheer himself up for the following day.

'Reg, you look very bitter today,' Nina said as she was washing the dishes and looking over her shoulder to see the melancholic Reginald sitting upon the bed.

'Could you turn the music off, please?' he said as he looked scornfully at the small radio, which was emitting jazzy tunes.

'Of course,' Nina quickly did as she was asked but remained inquisitive. 'Is everything all right?'

'Someone once said that you should never listen to cheerful music when you are sad, for it will only make you more so. Hope only lies in depressing music because somehow it provides an escape from the source of your own problem as it creates an entirely different problem that you can think about.' When Reginald saw how puzzled Nina looked, he simplified this by saying, 'Jazz just seems too upbeat for me right now.'

He stood up from the bed and approached her, taking her into his hands and giving her a kiss on the cheek.

'I'll go home early tonight.'

Mmm, she nodded, and he immediately appreciated her for being so understanding. However, once she was in his arms, he did not want to let go of her.

Later, when she was falling asleep softly in his embrace, Reginald placed small kisses on the back of her neck. At that moment, he knew that none of his characters could ever feel as alive as he did just then. Yet he still got up, got dressed and went back to his solitary apartment.

*

A powerfully radiant day had once more graced Reginald's existence. The spotless black suit was laid out upon his bed, and, as he looked at it, he felt just as a little child, impatiently awaiting the desired moment. He slicked back his hair with pomade and put on the suit. Looking in the mirror, he could not be prouder of what he had achieved.

When he had returned to his apartment the previous night, still painfully dissatisfied with his impersonation, Reginald had turned to his book of clippings of each of the characters he wanted to portray at some point in his life, for he had to ensure that the following day he would become someone vivacious and exciting. The page turned to him as if it was destined to, and Reginald was certain that this was the right choice. It was Ed Wood as portrayed by Johnny Depp in Tim Burton's film since this had been one of his favourite characters when he was younger. This was because he found the sheer undying optimism with which the outlandish screenwriter, director, producer, actor, author and film editor approached life to be truly inspiring. And what also pleased him was that he knew the film by heart and that his outward appearance required so little effort because he simply needed to iron his suit and retrieve the pomade from the back of his bathroom cabinet. The rest would come naturally from his acting skills, limited as they were, and his strong desire to be this particular character.

Reginald made a cup of strong black coffee and lay down upon his bed. It was still too early to go to work. His excitement had overtaken him so he had risen earlier than needed. He sipped his coffee and thought about his life. It was one of the rare moments where he allowed himself to delve into the chaos that was his existence, given the fact that he wasn't one person but several. His current lifestyle stemmed partly from his experience through his younger years in both school and university. While he had remained the same throughout these years, painfully discontent with himself, everybody around him changed. Their more mediocre traits and attitudes seemed to vanish overnight while Reginald could not recognise even the slightest shift in himself. So eventually, once everything in his life had come together and he finally needed to unburden his repressed emotions, he began to seek a constant transformation in himself.

He soon dismissed these thoughts because he was never fond of remembering the old him. Reginald now turned to Nina. Every character he embodied loved her dearly, and he knew that it was very unlikely that would change. But still, Reginald felt a desperate need to shield her from his daily routine. For as much as she was dear to him, he knew that she was an unnecessary distraction and that she was a link to the real world, and he feared beyond all else that she would eventually submit him to her and ensure that he became his true self. Of course, these thoughts were all irrational, but Reginald was not a person who saw things as they were or realistically might be. The future always held the worst scenario, the past was a chain of humiliating events, and the present was unpredictable and not entirely positive.

Reginald decided to smoke the last of his cigarettes while eating his minimalistic breakfast, which consisted of soup from a tin. The smoke seemed to cloud his mind as well as the air around him, and he rejoiced in the early morning calm and the sound of the few cars he heard passing his building outside. The phone rang annoyingly, with the sound frightening him.

'Reg?' Hearing Nina's voice made him smile.

'Yes?'

'Can we meet in the café today? For lunch, that is.'

'I can't make lunch; I won't have that long of a break.'

'Fine. After work then.'

'I'll see you there at six.'

Nina hung up immediately. This inexplicable call terrified Reginald because she rarely called him.

Ed Wood went to work and was admired for his outstanding optimism throughout the day. Everything was 'perfect' to him, and no mishaps pestered him, but a shadow obscured the lightness of his spirit. His fear of Nina's call did have a positive effect however, because now Reginald was absolutely sure that he was in love with her.

*

Nina took off her apron and joined Reginald at the table by the window. She removed magazines and newspapers from the windowsill to make space for herself. Reginald watched her attentively. His fingers constantly tried to loosen the collar of his shirt as Nina's slow movements, and unaffected manner made him worry all the more.

'Who are you today?' she asked.

'Ed Wood. Film director and so much more,' Reginald said, while he tried to maintain a steady hand to sip his coffee. 'He's a personal inspiration.'

'That's lovely, Reg.'

They sat in silence for a moment, both of them watching the rain drizzle on the hurrying people outside. Nina pulled at the ends of her hair.

'Reg, I wanted to see you because I have to talk to you about something.'

'Nina, you're scaring me,' he said this with a smile, trying not to lose his character.

She sighed breathlessly and then continued, 'I've been seeing someone else. And I feel terrible about it because I do love you. So I didn't know what to do, and I went to a fortune-teller. I've known the woman for years and have gone to her many times. She's very old; I don't think she'll live for much longer, she's already lost one leg. She's also very wise, and each time she has predicted something, it has been terribly accurate. So that is the problem, you see. She almost blatantly told me that we shouldn't be together because she saw no conceivable future for us because she believes that I will never find the stability and comfort that I am looking for with you. If anybody else had said it, I wouldn't have believed them, but her constant accuracy frightened me because I had been thinking the same thing for some time now.'

Reginald was speechless, turning the teaspoon in his cup.

'Yesterday, when you came over, I felt like you were a ghost. I did not feel like I could ever talk to you, to seek comfort from you because I would never know what reaction I could expect from whatever character it was you were portraying. Why can't we just be ourselves? Why can't you just like yourself?' Nina said, her voice breaking.

'I don't know,' his eyes could not meet hers. 'And you're entirely decided on this?'

'Unfortunately yes, Reggie.'

'It fascinates me how the roles have reversed. All along, I thought I was the unreasonable one, but it turns out that you're strange as well.'

'It's not very uncommon…'

'Oh, but it is. You're letting an ordinary human determine one of your life choices. Can that be taken lightly? Can it be considered as acceptable? How should it resonate with me? After all, this woman has now impacted my life as well. Not only that but you've also been seeing someone else.'

'Reg, I'm so sorry. I just don't see this working out in the long run. Let us just part as friends. I know that in your heart you see that this wasn't meant to last either. While with you every day is like an explosion of unpredictability, it is not what I am looking for when it comes to the future.'

'There's not much more to say. I'll just have to accept it then,' Reggie said, trying to ignore his heartbreak and remain focused on his character. Trying desperately to not betray his optimistic essence. 'So how was your day?' He smiled, the everlasting smile which Ed Wood seemed to possess and sipped his coffee meticulously. It seemed like he had been waiting for her to say the words that he could not say and, now that she had, there was no longer any point in trying to turn back time.

Nina raised her eyebrow in disbelief but did not wish to protest. 'Not too bad.'

'I'm glad to hear that,' he said as Nina gave him a forced smile and, placing her elbows on the table, rested her chin upon her hands.

'Will you come by every so often?' she said, biting her lip, trying to hold back tears.

'You know that I fell for this place long ago, so out of respect for my close relationship with this establishment, I think that I must come by,' Reginald winked playfully. 'Say do you have some pie today?'

'Peach or blueberry?'

'Peach would be perfect.'

Nina turned to go and he saw how much he had hurt her just now by remaining true to his self of the day.

*

The ash descended upon the windowsill in silent crumbs. Did it even matter if Heathcliff smoked or not? His unwashed hair moved ever so slightly in the breeze. Yes, these details did matter to Reginald, however, he couldn't force himself to care about that since he could not overpower the intruder who had found his way into his heart. Sanity, if one could call it that. Even as Heathcliff, he no longer felt like himself. As Heathcliff yearned for his Catherine, Reginald now thought only of Nina. It was close to dusk, and he had not eaten for the entire day. Food now seemed entirely irrelevant, a mere frivolity, just as it had been for poor Heathcliff who starved, possessed by the ghost of Catherine.

There was nothing else to do but start anew. Only by now, Reginald had understood that whatever form he could take, no one would ever fully accept him. Not truly, at least, because it would be inevitable that they would sense that they are only receiving a small part of that person. More than that, Reginald had so much love for Nina, and he knew that it wasn't going to go anywhere since it wasn't the kind of thing that he could exchange and give to another person. Reginald was at a loss at how he could remedy this. There is really no explanation given as to how a person who truly despises every aspect of themselves can lead an average and happy life and find true love. Reginald was repulsed by his own looks, the limitations that weighed down on his intelligence, and his chaotic character, which was also a distinct flaw. He couldn't bear the thought that if he were to form a relationship, some other person would have to wake up next to such a miserable being. Since, without his many masks, he was a blank canvas in every shape and form, the only thing painted upon it being a dark and revolting stroke of distaste for oneself. There was one thing left to try, but he knew that it was his last resort, and if this did not work out, he would be lost forever.

*

The day smelt of sandalwood and oak. He walked up the steps to the apartment building and pressed down on the button, feeling his body shiver with a wave of uncertainty. The building was neat and precise, just as everything else in the lives of the people who lived in this neighbourhood. The intercom was turned on, and a confident voice spoke, 'Yes, who is it?'

'It's Reginald.'

'Reg? That can't be you! Come on up.'

The buzzer was the sound of a pleasant bird cooing. Reginald opened the door doubtfully, and, as he stared at the immaculate marble staircase, he knew he had made a terrible mistake. He was not worthy of this place. Many years ago, he had made a true friend. A friend who could understand him and identify with his problems but, as the years passed and Reginald distanced himself from modern society, they failed to keep in touch. Unconsciously he did make his way up the staircase and found Gabriel in front of his door, smiling without a hint of feigning.

'Reginald! How are you, friend? You look slightly drunk,' he laughed. Reginald would never reveal that he was portraying Don Draper from *Mad Men* at that very moment, and so he had had quite a few drinks before coming over. 'Come in!' Gabriel ushered him in before giving him a heartfelt brotherly hug.

He opened the door to an elaborate apartment where the walls were concealed with wallpaper with an elegant Fleur de Lis pattern, and each piece of furniture seemed to possess years upon years of life experience.

'Whiskey or brandy?'

'Whiskey has always been my poison,' Reginald said, still in awe of his surroundings.

Gabriel handed him the drink and sat down on one of the sofas, gesturing to the other one for Reginald to take a seat.

Sitting opposite Gabriel was intimidating because Reginald knew with the utmost certainty that Gabriel was in every way superior to him. Yet, he knew that a man of that sort would always uphold the vows of true friendship, practically sealed by blood in university days.

'So, Reg, why have I not heard from you in so terribly long? I did try to look for you, imploring your parents to give me your address but they didn't seem to know it either.'

'I have been living a rather secluded life, off the grid.'

'Is it because of your, you know, strange tendencies?'

'Yes,' Reggie said after a moment's hesitation.

'Well, you look rather average now. Are you still wrapped up in that?'

This was when Reginald had to decide whether to betray his entire being to go through with what he saw as rehabilitation or just reveal himself for what it truly was. He chose the former.

'No. That is why I came here. I've found a reasonable job here in the city, but I live quite far out, so I would have to commute for three hours each day. Since I will earn good money, I was wondering, if you could help out an old friend and let me stay with you for a short while, rent a room, until I can find a place of my own nearer the workplace.'

Gabriel smiled as if this was what he was expecting; 'Of course, you can, Reg. To be honest, I'd been waiting for you to come to your senses for a while now,' he gulped down his whiskey sour. 'You didn't go through the horror of studying to become an accountant just to find yourself sectioned years later, which it would have come to eventually. Your fascination with playing dress-up was not normal by any means.'

Gabriel continued talking. This was what Reginald had always liked about him. He could fade into the background and just be whoever he was that day without actually having to do anything, without having to act. There was no job. However, his intentions were true. He did hope that if he were to live in this reality, amongst people who were considered to conform to the standard of the social norm, he would cure himself of his need to be different people all in one.

*

For the first time in years, Reginald awoke to the sound of wind rushing through the trees in the garden below rather than the noise of cars. A sound of silence. His steps towards the bathroom remained cautious and unsure because he was still not fully awake and feared that at any point, due to a sudden movement, this magnificent illusion of luxury and comfort would shatter. However, it did not, and after he had rinsed his face with cold water, he felt invigorated.

Gabriel had left a suit on his door. Truthfully, he didn't know if it had been Gabriel himself or a housemaid, but Reginald had no choice but to wear it. It worked in his favour because he knew that this was one of Gabriel's suits, so it made it easier for him to embody Gabriel all the more. The clothes, the surroundings, listening to his way with words and absorbing Gabriel's confidence; everything seemed to be there to help him become someone normal. However, even though Reginald continued the same impersonation for weeks, the personality change was soon noticed by Gabriel. Mostly because they had a lot of evenings out together to elite clubs, and it must have become obvious to Gabriel that something was not quite right since their conversations seemed to verge on the bizarre, with Gabriel feeling as though he was talking to a mirror. The confrontation came one mediocre evening.

Reginald returned home from a bar. He walked through the living room and found himself at the door of his bedroom. The door was slightly ajar, and after Reginald had entered the room, he understood why. Gabriel was sitting on one of the easy chairs in the corner of the room, the light touching his face, which showed mistrust and disappointment. It was like something out of a film.

'Reg, sit down.' He had no choice but to sit down on the immaculately made bed, for to sit down on the other chair in such close proximity to Gabriel would have been deeply awkward.

'You never had any intention of giving this up, did you? You lied to me of all people. Because you knew that I wouldn't be able to understand. You were completely right. I don't. This childish obsession is destroying your life. It's like you're a junkie. But these characters that you impersonate, that sustain you, I don't know any of them. I knew Reginald, and he was a friend, a damn good one at that, but he isn't there any more.'

Reginald didn't know how he had figured it out. Maybe due to his poor acting skills and the fact that Gabriel was so unlike him. There was nothing to do now but admit the truth.

'This has always been me, Gabe. I was like this at university, and you knew it. If you never accepted that, then I suppose we were never friends in the first place. I have tried to live a regular life, but I just can't. I can't conform to your standards. To me, it's torture. The monotony of it all. What boring lives regular people must lead,' Reginald sighed and got up because he saw that his words only made Gabriel more irritated. 'I did not want to disappoint you, and I certainly did not want to abuse your kindness, but I had nowhere else to go, and I really thought that staying with you might help with this, but it hasn't.'

'I'm sorry, Reg, but you can't stay here any more. You need to create a life for yourself; you can't expect others to string you along and support you.'

Reginald smiled as a sign of gratitude for what Gabriel had done for him all the same and then left the apartment.

*

After this scene, Reginald felt strangely empowered. Every night that he had gone to sleep at Gabriel's place, he had done so with the sincere belief that the following morning he would be himself, but he never was. Yet now, for the first time in years, he saw his trait as a diversity that others lacked. Drawing strength from this revelation, he made his way from the city's tidy and refined side to the shabby neighbourhood where Nina lived. Passion filled his veins, and he felt it warm his blood in the most pleasurable way. He wanted to put his head on her chest and listen to the low thumping melody of her heart. His lips missed the touch of hers. He knew that she would bring sense back into his life and that she would make him feel fine about being himself again.

These thoughts rushed in his mind until he found himself standing at her door, but then he stopped his feverish dreams. He wasn't himself and never would be, and he knew that he could not ring the doorbell. He understood that a relationship required something which he lacked, namely consistency. For all the exciting and brilliant stories about couples who based their lives on spontaneous moments, he knew that everyday life was not like that. That was only the beginning of any relationship, but Nina and he no longer had that, so his impulsive lifestyle became a nuisance rather than a pleasant surprise. He had failed in his attempt to become who she wanted him to be and, even though he wanted her to open the door so that he could tell her how much he had missed her and how much he loved her, Reginald knew that this would be meaningless because she would not know who was saying it to her.

The Sleep Itch

'Never in my life would I have thought that I could say that I can build a tent. Quite easily, at that,' Adriana said as she packed away the last of her stuff.

'I know. Skills! Which we can use for next year,' Emma said proudly and smiled at Paul.

'So you guys are up for coming to this festival next year?'

'Yes. I think I mentioned before how much I hate festivals but this was so much fun. I am actually sad that we're leaving.'

'I think you did mention it a couple of times,' Paul chuckled. Adriana had told them all about how Emma used to drag her to festivals when they were teenagers and about the horrible time she'd had there. However, now as she looked at her surroundings from the green plains all around them, the bright stalls and tents in the distance where they'd danced their hearts out and all the way to the forest where they had found a hidden cave entirely covered in crystals and had turned it into a mini rave, this particular festival was bound to leave behind a wealth of positive memories. The company also helped. Adriana and Emma had not seen Paul and his friends for a while and they had been a breath of fresh air. It reminded them of their university days as they had been to the best events with Paul since he always knew how to find them.

They had packed up all of their things and made their way to the car so that Paul could drive them to the train station. As the car drove away from the festival site, Adriana was once again reminded that they had in fact been in the middle of the nowhere for three days. They drove for two hours before they reached the first town. By that time, the trio were hungry and they stopped at a McDonald's drive-thru, where they ordered too much food. Paul then drove them to the coast which was minutes away and they found a spot on the beach with a majestic bridge and rippling water. They ate their food there, while Emma constantly took pictures of the scenery and the three of them. She was always the best at capturing moments. Adriana was grateful for that because she knew that she would want to remember this particular one. In fact, she did not want it to end but even more than that, she did not want to return to reality.

*

Adriana left the train station feeling confused. She was carrying three heavy bags and was now actually feeling hungover; not so much from the alcohol, as from the weekend itself. She had said goodbye to Paul and Emma, and had made her way back to her home town. When she left the bustle of the station and entered the car park, she saw Jake's car in the distance.

'Hello, can you open the car boot please?' Adriana said as she came up to the car window.

'Hey! Of course.'

She chucked all of her stuff in there and got in the car.

'Hello again.'

'Hi,' he leaned in to give her a kiss on the cheek.

'I thought you'd be in the train station. I looked everywhere for you. I would have called but my phone is completely out of battery,' Adriana said in a reproachful tone.

'Oh, sorry. I assumed you'd find me.'

'It's fine, no worries.'

He started the car and they made their way home. Adriana was not in the best of moods and she was aware of it, yet something still felt off. It seemed like the city had lost a bit of its colour and that Jake had become even colder. They drove in silence and Adriana could not stand it.

'I had an amazing time. I feel like I've discovered so many new bands. And the weather was perfect, which we were kind of worried about initially. There were so many interesting hippie events there every day. Also it was so nice to see Emma and Paul. We've pretty much decided that we will go there next year too. It's just too good. Maybe you'll join us then.'

'We'll see. You know I'm not into events like that though.'

'I know. I'm not either, however I loved this one.'

Since he did not ask any further questions, they continued their drive in silence. Once they got back to the apartment, Adriana put away all of her things and went for a shower. It was so nice to feel clean after feeling like a mess for days, however she had hoped Jake would join her. She should have known better.

Adriana got into bed and texted Emma and Paul, letting them know that she got home safely. She thanked Paul once again for suggesting this event and promised that she would join him next year. Jake was in the other room watching a TV show, so she decided to go to sleep.

*

It was five in the morning when Adriana awoke with a start. There was a lump in her throat and she knew she would not be able to sleep again since she would not willingly go back to the nightmare she had had. Tiptoeing out of the room, she made sure not to wake Jake. There was a mustard yellow glow in the air as the sky was covered in ominous dark clouds, yet it seemed as though the sun was trying to peek through them. She made her coffee and went to the living room with her dream journal. Adriana could not help but notice that she was scratching the back of her neck excessively. As she started recounting her dream, the pit in her stomach grew.

In the dream, Jake had bought a giant apartment and asked her to move in with him and she had accepted the offer. However, she did find it strange that he had bought it on his own without even consulting her. They moved in and she started unpacking, however Jake decided to invite everyone he knew over so the apartment soon turned into a mess and Adriana was hopelessly trying to tidy it all up, meanwhile getting lost in the many rooms and the twists and turns of the place. She never seemed to end up in the same room twice. Suddenly, clouds of birds started attacking the house, breaking through the windows, trying to squeeze themselves under the door and dying in the process, however the ones who made it through managed to attack several of Jake's friends, some of whom died from their wounds. Adriana just hid in one of the many rooms and by the time the birds left, it seemed as though there would be nothing left to salvage in their apartment. There was a mess of blood, guts, feathers and corpses everywhere, a stain on their new start. Her dream journal had a prompt for each entry asking, 'What do you think this dream is trying to tell you?' But Adriana often left it empty. Sometimes she really did not want to even entertain the thought.

*

'Morning, how did you sleep?'

Jake shuffled into the kitchen with cautious steps, sleep still weighing down his eyelids. Adriana pushed away her coffee cup and looked up at him.

'Not well.'

'Oh no, why?'

'I had a nightmare.'

She got up to put her cup in the sink. She had already had three coffees and it was only nine in the morning.

'It was basically Hitchcock's "The Birds" scenario except somehow even worse. I was in this huge apartment and—'

'Not now, hun. I've just woken up. I don't think I can deal with whatever horror movie scenario you went through.'

'True, no worries. There's some fresh coffee in the French press. I have to get back to work.'

'Okay, thanks.'

Although she felt rejected, Adriana pushed this feeling away and went to her home office to return to her documents, which she had tried to look at all morning but had made little progress on. Her mind was clearly preoccupied and it did not help that Jake had brushed her off when she really needed to talk her nightmare through with someone. She kept scratching at her neck and then suddenly pulled her hand away.

'Jake, can you come here for a second?'

'Sure,' it took him a while to show up. 'What is it?'

'Can you please have a look at the back of my neck? It's so itchy. Is there something there?'

'Yes, there are three red bumps. Probably mosquitoes.'

'Ugh, I hate mosquito season. Have you been bitten?'

'Nope, all good for now, thank God.'

'Lucky.' She turned around and smiled at him. Adriana

pushed her body into his. Her silky pyjamas slid across his skin.

'Someone's feeling frisky,' Jake laughed.

'Is that a bad thing?'

'I've hardly woken up.'

'You look pretty awake to me.'

'Come on, Adriana, stop. Another time, okay?'

She nodded.

Jake gave her a kiss on the forehead and left the room. Adriana sat down in her chair but felt like she could not sit still. She made her way to the bathroom where she sat down on the side of the bathtub and cried.

*

Another five a.m. start. Another nightmare. Adriana had dealt with nightmares before however they had rarely been as vivid as the ones she had experienced over the last few days. She had also woken up partly because of scratching herself as she noticed that there were now tiny red bumps all along her arms and legs. For a moment she thought that she might have to go to sleep the following night with oven mitts taped to her hands, because while she was still sleeping she felt like she might tear off her skin. She once again made her way to the kitchen for coffee with her dream journal in hand.

This nightmare had started off with her and Patrick, her ex-boyfriend, on a boat. They were moving in an unknown direction and Adriana could tell how distraught he was. The two of them had been together only for a short amount of time, however she had cared about him a lot. However, she could tell that it was not meant to be. Patrick kept telling her that he wished her the best and that he would always be there if she needed him. He also promised to design her wedding dress. As they sailed, Patrick worked on the dress and Adriana yearned to see Jake. The boat docked at the small seaside town where Adriana had spent most of her childhood. She descended from the boat in a flowy and glittering gown, only to be greeted by people she did not recognise. They all seemed to be Jake's friends so that the only familiar face to her was Patrick. The dock was decorated with white wilting flowers and chains of lights, some of which had gone out. When she turned around to seek reassurance from Patrick, he was gone. She approached Jake at the altar and once she was there, the priest began the ceremony. When he asked Adriana whether she would take Jake as her husband she gave the latter a shy look before saying her 'I do'. However, when the priest asked Jake, he pulled Adriana close to him and drove a blade through her stomach, slashing her open, decorating her dress with her entrails. He then took her in his arms and carried her to a pit not far from the altar where he threw her on a pile of other bodies; those of her family and friends.

When Adriana finished writing down her dream, she realised that she had cried throughout writing it. The wave of emotion she felt about what had happened overtook her entirely. It felt as though she had not slept whatsoever as her dream life seemed even more active than her real one. More so, this dream seemed to predict something horrifying and she did not know if she even wanted to let those thoughts near her. The exhaustion was getting to her and she couldn't stop scratching her bug bites. Adriana was convinced that it was not mosquitoes. Not only had she not seen or heard any the last couple of nights, but the fact that Jake remained unaffected by it indicated that it might be something else. She turned to Google and, after she had ruled out skin rashes, started looking up any potential news about bugs in the area or anything that matched her situation. Several possible answers came up, along with suggestions of what might help.

The moment Jake was out of bed, Adriana threw the sheets in the wash, along with the pillows, the blanket, the clothes she had been wearing and the curtains that were hanging in the bedroom. She hoovered the room from top to bottom, paying special attention to the mattress.

'Is this really necessary?' Jake asked, observing her with a look of concern and derision.

'It's the only thing I can think to do. We'll also not open the window here for the next few days. Possible culprits are harvest mites or berry bugs or something like that so there's no way to see them because they are miniscule. Just have to hope that now that I've washed every cloth-like material here, it might help.'

'It's just weird that I haven't been bit at all.'

'I know. It's not fair.'

'You really should go to the pharmacy and buy some cream or something for those bites. You've been scratching them too much.' Jake shrugged and walked away.

*

Later that evening, Adriana found herself in the kitchen preparing food. It felt like the entire day had slipped away from her. She was tired, angry and trying desperately not to pay attention to the bug bites. She had just cooked a piece of steak and as she was slicing it and the blood-like juice was seeping out onto the cutting board she couldn't help but think where else the bugs might be. Maybe they were everywhere. In the food they ate, the towels she used, the sofas in the living room. Maybe it was would be best to just set the whole apartment on fire. Jake poked his head through the kitchen door.

'How long until food?'

'It's ready. Just have to plate it.'

'What are we having tonight?'

'Steak, fries and salad.'

'I feel like we had that not too long ago. Do you ever think about experimenting with recipes?'

Adriana ignored what he said; the answer required too much energy, which she couldn't spare at the moment. Instead, she gave him his plate and he went to the living room to continue watching his TV show. Adriana stayed in the kitchen. She sat down at the table and poured herself a large glass of wine. She hoped that this might help her fall asleep.

A few hours later, Adriana was reading a book in bed, trying to focus on the story before her rather than scratching. Despite being hyper-focused, she felt herself getting lost in the words before her and she had to read many of the sentences several times. Even though she couldn't see the bugs, she was sure she felt them scurry across her skin. At around one o'clock, Jake joined her in bed. He turned off the light and began scrolling through a news site on his phone. Adriana put down her book and cuddled up to him. She placed her hand on his chest, feeling the slow rhythm of his breath. Her palm slid downward but he stopped her before she got to where she was aiming for.

'Hey, hey. Don't give me your harvest mites.'

'Excuse me?'

'I'm just teasing you, hun,' he laughed and kissed her hair. 'I'm just too tired. It's been a long week. Also it's just far too hot in this room. I wish we could open the window.'

'I want to see if that makes a difference so the window stays closed for tonight,' Adriana snapped. 'I can't live like this!'

'What do you mean?'

She knew what she wanted to say and what she actually meant, however, Adriana just replied, 'I need sleep. I've been dealing with nightmares that wake me up for days now and I'm scratching myself to death every night. It's just too much.'

'I know, hun. I wish I could help.'

'Yeah, me too,' Adriana said as she turned off the light on her side of the bed and closed her eyes.

Her friend Millie had gone on a romantic weekend retreat with her husband and had entrusted her two little girls to Adriana. She spoiled them rotten; giving them sweets, playing *Animal Crossing* with them for hours and watching every single episode of *Masha and the Bear* she could find. The girls were due a bath and as she put them in the warm bubbly water with their favourite cotton candy coloured duck, she noticed that the moment she put her hand towards them, their bodies seemed to disappear until the two of them simply dissolved, becoming one with the bath water. She realised the children were dead and that she was responsible. Adriana grasped at the water but there was nothing there. She noticed that her arm was covered in a rash and as she reached the mirror, she saw that there were bumps all over her neck and chest area.

She awoke and wanted to scream. Rushing to the bathroom, she checked in the mirror and she indeed had new bumps on her, which she had been scratching while asleep. The entire area from her neck to her chest and stomach was red and blotchy. At this point, the only part of her that was spared from this affliction was her face. She returned to bed and sat there until the sun came up and Jake opened his eyes.

'This is getting ridiculous. I don't understand what's happening.'

'I think you should go to the doctor today, if you can. You really don't look good, hun.'

'I have too much work to do today and we have that early dinner booked.'

'Oh, I completely forgot about that.'

'Me too,' Adriana said, forcing a smile.

*

'Are you going to have some wine?'

'No, I'm good. Will just have water,' Jake said, looking off into the distance.

Adriana scanned the menu and realised that she was not hungry at all, even though everything looked nice. She wore her long flowery dress, to hide as much of herself as possible. She looked over at Jake and could tell that he did not want to be there. Although he would never say it outright, she knew that he would rather be at home. Yet they had just arrived at the restaurant and they still had both dinner and a film ahead of them. They had agreed on a monthly date night, following an argument started by Adriana during which she had brought up how lonely she felt and how much she yearned for them to just be a normal couple again, cliché romantics and all. Despite the bad feeling Adriana sensed when it came to the evening, the night passed quite smoothly. They had their dinner, went to the cinema, saw their mystery-thriller and went back to their apartment.

As Adriana walked to the kitchen to get a glass of water, Jake went to the bedroom. She soon followed him and saw that he had put on his pyjamas.

'I don't know why I'm so tired. Fridays take on a different feel once you start getting older, huh?' he said, climbing into bed.

When he said things like this it made him sound so ancient that Adriana had to keep reminding herself that they were both still in their early thirties. She lay down next to him and took his face in her hands.

'It's all about perception. We can still make it fun.'

'I mean, if you want to.'

'I do,' she bit her lip and continued looking at him, waiting for him to make a move.

'Well, do something. You're the one who came here!' Jake suddenly seemed to snap, raising his voice slightly.

'Oh, wow.'

'That sounded wrong.'

'No, it's fine. I understand,' Adriana said as she moved off the bed. She rushed to the bathroom. Throughout the evening she had almost forgotten about the unbearable itching that plagued her. But now that she was there, she just let go. Scratching every single spot on her skin, she didn't give a damn, so that when she started seeing blood she didn't feel like she could stop. The release felt too precious. She stayed there for what felt like hours and emerged from the bathroom tear-stained and covered in bleeding bites. Blood trickled down her arms and legs onto the sheets as she got into bed and placed her arms around Jake's sleeping body for one last time.

Mutual Attraction

For Stuart

The field was quiet. The fog rolled in over the scattered trees in the distance. A lonely scarecrow stood firmly next to the crops, looking as though it was contemplating its existence. Crickets everywhere, yet they remain unseen. The day was coming to an end. The setting sun shone in his eyes, the wind gently lifted his unkempt hair, while the ants crawled along the stones placed around the crackling fire. At times such as this, Noah had no doubts about the decision he had made because he was finally not robbed of these little pleasures. Over the slight hill in the distance, the sky began to dress itself in the colours of apricot and amber, melting into the darker tones of indigo and scarlet. There will be rain tomorrow, Noah thought, as in his childhood, his grandmother had repeatedly told him that a colourful sky meant rain or snow. He had always failed to take note of how true this was.

He had quit his job a week ago. Meanwhile, three weeks ago, he had been violently ill. It started as an excruciating sore throat, but when it did not go away, and his temperature kept climbing, he went to the doctor, who told him that it was a recurrence of glandular fever that he'd suffered as a child. The doctor also told him that this can only happen in one of two cases, either when the person is immunocompromised or under extreme stress. Noah fell into the latter category, and as the doctor was telling him that he had caused his own illness, the fear which began to creep into his heart became terrifying. After lying in bed for two weeks, drifting off to sleep every couple of hours and fighting off the fever which he kept succumbing to, he knew that something in his life had to change. In his case that required little imagination as he merely quit his job, left the city and drove to his parents' house in the countryside. They had both moved abroad, and Noah rarely saw them as he was too afraid to get on a plane to go and visit them. However, his mother continuously sent him uplifting messages about not taking work too seriously or trying to encourage him to go out and do things but, try as he might, Noah could only appreciate the sentiment and never embrace the idea behind them.

    Upon coming inside, he went to the kitchen and set his cup on the light wood table, which had the round marks of hot cups imprinted on it from his childhood. He shuffled upstairs to the bedroom. The sheets were perfectly ironed, clear and lacy white, a remnant and staple of his mother's touch in this house. Small moths jumped against the net taped over the window as they desperately tried to reach the light inside. Noah walked up to the stacked shelves near the bed and lightly passed his hand over the hundreds of empty perfume bottles neatly arranged in rows. Some were slightly dusty as they were impossible to clean but his mother kept them beautifully preserved behind the glass pane. It had been his mother's obsession, which had begun when she was young. Collecting perfumes and keeping the bottles once the last drop was gone meant that she could preserve the art itself. Some are so intricately designed that it would be a crime to throw them away. Noah opened one of them and breathed in the strong scent of Vanderbilt which was conserved in a flat bottle with a transparent swan on it. It was as though his childhood was also in these bottles. His mother's scent brought back pleasant memories of his own innocence and carefree nature.

Noah closed his eyes under the covers and tried to think of anything outside the frame of his present life, but it appeared as though everything he could imagine worried him equally. In the evening, there is always a clear feeling, and for Noah, this was a wave of determination as he understood that he needed to improve his life. This feeling usually dies with the rising sun, and so the following morning, he had lost all ability to persevere with his plans. This was an endless cycle.

*

A car drove along the road sending a wave of dust across the pure green field. The wave halted just before it reached the garden where Noah lay on a wool blanket sipping crushed berries with hot water. Only birds kept him company as they sat on the apple tree branches above him, guarding him from the stillness. He thought that today might finally have to be the day that he visited his grandmother. It was early morning, the dew still hanging onto the grass around him, so he had plenty of time to muster up the courage he needed for that meeting if he was to go there at lunchtime. Noah stood up and folded the scratchy material.

He was soon in the car. On his way there, he stopped at the local supermarket and bought five bags of chocolate candy, for his grandmother had a sweet tooth like no other, and a container of the cheapest coffee which was the only type the old lady drank. As he drove past the many bus stops scattered along the patchy road, Noah noticed that at many of them, teenagers were sitting and drinking alcohol from bottles blatantly hidden in paper bags, although nobody would have cared anyway. He had remarked upon this many times before because it seemed to be a custom in the around these parts, but only now did he realise how sad it was. It was as though these young people were waiting for a bus to take them away from the dreary boredom of the countryside. Still, instead of actually leaving, they were only drinking away their lives in the place which represented that potential. Noah averted his eyes and instead, looked at the road before him, at the faded white line swallowed by the car. Suddenly, everything before him disappeared, and the only thing he could see before his eyes was a bright light. Slowly, soft lines emerged before him and what appeared was a never-ending Excel sheet, numbers upon numbers appearing in the table. He blinked, and yet it was still there. With caution, Noah veered to the side of the road, or where he thought it would be, and stopped the car. The table kept scrolling in front of him, senseless information attacking him. He sat still, shut his eyes as tight as he could and waited for it to stop. Time passed unknowingly, and when he finally opened them, it was no longer there, just the same empty road before him with a bus stop not far away, where two young men were sitting, pointing at him and laughing because Noah had tears running down his cheeks. He started the car, and as it rolled forwards, he tried to fight off the horror that seeped into his heart.

At noon, still shaken, he drove into the deep emerald shade of the forest, following an uneven hardly-there road. A small brick house came into view in a clearing encircled by tall pines. Outside it was a metallic table, by which a black furry dog was sniffing about. His fur was so thick and overgrown that it was difficult to tell his face from his rear end. Noah got out of the tiny car and stretched his aching muscles. The door opened, and a well-built old lady appeared. Her grey hair, which still hid some chestnut streaks, was tied back with a lilac scarf, her hands gripped her sides as she stood stoically and watched him approach. Once a convinced communist, his grandmother had become a convinced and active nationalist fighting for independence in the later years of her life. However, the problem was that people bored her. They always seemed to be doing everything incorrectly or were just plain stupid, so she had left her political activism and had gone to live in the middle of a forest by herself. Fortunately, that had happened after Noah had grown up as his grandmother had been an essential part of his childhood. Taking him to basketball training, kindergarten, and school, she had always been around, willing to do everything for him but remaining stern and strict. She inspired him since she had the character of someone who could not be overthrown by even the toughest of wars and who would never succumb to the routine imposed by society.

'Noah,' his grandmother put her arms around him and placed a wet kiss on his cheek. 'You're late. I made lunch two hours ago. You're lucky I didn't feed it all to Artemis.' The dog, upon hearing his name, sprinted towards them and, as Noah stroked the mutt's head, he pressed to his legs affectionately.

'Ah, what a good little dog you are, how lovely you are,' encouraged by his grandmother's words Artemis jumped up, placing his paws on the old lady's shoulders, 'Get off me, silly buffoon!' The familiar sternness emerged with a confident and overpowering voice. Noah laughed as the dog rushed away behind a bush, tail between his legs.

They went inside, Noah carrying the things that he had bought at the store. He sighed as he was once again forced to see the minuscule kitchen, the cramped living room, the overall state of the lodgings of his misanthropic grandmother. The rooms were filled with the strong and cosy scent of mushroom sauce. Noah raised the lid of the pan on the stove. It was his childhood favourite. This sauce and potatoes, as well as pancakes with sugar, had been all he had lived on.

At the table in the living room, Noah hunched beneath a shelf as his grandmother put a hearty amount of food on their plates before she started talking about all of her crops and flowers. The rate they grew at, what she would do for next year, which things she would pack and give to Noah, every single detail needed to be discussed with a serious approach. Meanwhile, Noah's eyes drifted over the room until, with an adorable pang, he noticed the little cabinet upon which his grandmother had gathered a multitude of family pictures. His own cheerful face stared back at him. A small child on rollerblades rushing towards the camera with a dog-like smile, wearing a navy-blue sweater and black corduroy trousers, holding a stuffed animal. A zebra. Somehow this detail made Noah give way to a short laugh, for a zebra was somehow the perfect representation of his current existential crisis.

His grandmother's hands moved swiftly to pull away all the plates before she came back with a bowl of blueberries, then coffee, sugar and hot water. She poured the ground coffee into his cup, then poured the water onto it. She seemed to have forgotten about herself as she poured hot water into her own cup and then dumped the coffee in after it, the dark grounds floating upon the surface. Noah's eyes were fixed on her slightly trembling hands as she mixed the brew and added four teaspoons of sugar. The little brown spots on her hands had always seemed endearing to Noah, a sign of kindness. Every memory she was a part of made Noah feel certain envy because he was envious of himself for having experienced that moment. A moment which could not be grasped or held again. This realisation that his grandmother was, in fact, old and would not be with him for much longer sent him into a quiet cold sweat, and he tried to rush the rest of their time together as much as possible because he wanted to leave since he was too afraid that he would have an anxiety attack.

*

That night, with nothing but the melody of crickets to create a slight buzz outside, Noah woke up to stillness. He looked at the clock beside the bed. The numbers four-zero-zero glowed brightly red. Rousing his heavy limbs out of bed, he made his way to the bathroom. Everything in the house was asleep in the darkness. He moved along the corridor and suddenly stopped in his tracks as a loud and familiar sound could be heard from the living room. Slow, cautious steps led him towards it and there, in the dark, a large office printer was producing page after page of meaningless words. Noah sank down onto the sofa and watched it, feeling like he was being pulled back into the world that he was trying to escape.

Just a few months ago, he had been sitting like this, with the same sense of dread, in a doctor's office, awaiting the results of his monthly check-up. He'd been doing this for years, going to get blood tests and an occasional x-ray or ultrasound. There was never anything wrong, as the doctor repeatedly assured him there wouldn't be given that he didn't drink, didn't do drugs, didn't smoke, ate healthy food, worked out regularly and always made sure to get at least nine hours of sleep. Nevertheless, Noah was convinced that he would die before reaching old-age and was terrified of that. Therefore, when the doctor diagnosed his recurrence of glandular fever only a few weeks later, Noah almost felt a sense of triumph because he felt like he had been right. Although he avoided explicitly saying 'I told you so' to his doctor.

Sitting in the pale blue waiting room of the doctor's office, as he was then, always made his heart race with anxiety. He noticed an older woman come into the room and, as she sat down next to him, her eyes were so focused on Noah that he could not help but return the favour. Her hair was crow black with a white line gracing her parting, grey roots growing out. She was wearing a flamingo pink tracksuit and clutched one of those bags that Noah kept seeing wherever he went, Louis Vuitton or something like that. She was also holding a postcard in her hand with a smiling bunny on it, the word bubble saying, 'Thank you.' After a sigh, she leaned closer to Noah and spoke:

'Do you know that feeling when you go to the doctor's office, and you see all those cards and think to yourself: what are they supposed to do with them? Last time I was here, all I could do was stare at the cards on the windowsill, so I went home and tried to find the ones that people had given me and I couldn't. Then I realised that I had thrown them away. They were on my bookshelf and once, when I was cleaning, I just picked them up, not even stopping to think about the emotions expressed in them, and threw them out. What else are you supposed to do with them?'

Noah opened his mouth to answer but couldn't find anything to say. The woman then nodded quite seriously and added 'Exactly' before taking out a pen and starting to scribble a message on the bunny card in her hand. Only a moment later, Noah was called in to see the doctor, and although he vaguely heard him go through the results and assure him that everything was fine yet again, he couldn't stop looking at the rows of thank you cards on the windowsill. He wondered how long some of them had been there, how many of those people were still alive and, if they were, whether they still felt grateful. He thought about the woman and whether this was what she had thought too and why, having been so confused about what one was supposed to do with the cards, she still wanted to give one to the doctor. Maybe she wanted to do it as an experiment to see whether it would be displayed and, if so, for how long. Maybe she wanted to leave it there so that it would be something to remember her by, a sign that she had been there.

Noah awoke to silence once more. The printer had disappeared. The first bright rays of sunshine were creeping in through the parted curtains. He got up and went to make breakfast. Porridge, berries that he went out to pick from one of the bushes in the garden and some of the honey that his grandmother had given him, and a cup of coffee, as usual. He sat on the steps of the house, breathing in the crystal-clear morning air. The local stray cat from the nearby town came by to say hello, and Noah decided to use this moment of having a great listener by his side to talk about his thoughts.

'Why am I so afraid, tabby? Why has this been my life since I was little? I remember thinking as a kid that I would have that one decisive moment in my life. Like that moment from cartoons and movies where it would come down to me having to decide which colour wire to cut so that the bomb doesn't explode. That there would be some meaning in my death if I chose the wrong one, and if I got the right one, then anything beyond that point wouldn't matter because I would have done something incredible and death couldn't affect me any more. But it never came, and it never will. I realised I'd die in that job. A mere cog in the wheel of state bureaucracy. Not knowing why I was there, what I was doing and what it was for.'

The cat meowed as his hand had stopped stroking her. She got out of his lap, did a little shake and gave him an understanding look as if to say, what you're going through sounds tough, but I can't help you, and then quickly tip-tapped away. Noah continued sipping his coffee and tried to move his thoughts to something else. He already felt lighter having spoken to the cat. He ran through his tasks for the day, namely that he needed to cut the grass, pick redcurrants off quite a few bushes to bring them to his grandmother so that she could make jam, and he had to chop some more wood for the evening bonfire. He also had to go to the nearby shop to buy some food. It was a lot to do in one day, but at least he knew why he was doing it.

*

The meat had been marinating in vinegar, brown sugar, onions and herbs for quite a few hours, and so Noah finally brought it to the fire to cook it. He felt invigorated and yet satisfyingly tired. He had just had a shower after having spent the day mowing grass in the field that stretched alongside the house before starting the fire. His upper half was pleasantly bronzed from the touch of the sun, and he felt his arms ache from having used the scythe for hours on end.

A stork was walking gracefully through the field, looking for a sign of food. Upon seeing this, Noah's mind immediately went to its usual place. A symbol of life walking through the long-dead strands of grass he had cut earlier. More of it would grow soon, that being the way of things, and he found comfort in that. Knowing that his death would not really matter in the grand scheme of things, given that many more anxious creatures like him would be born and die after he was already gone. Sitting by the fire and watching the clementine sky slowly take over, he finally felt a sense of inner peace. He munched on a piece of cucumber and then on the chicken he'd prepared when suddenly he was forced to exclaim in pain as he had bitten into something hard and sharp. He pulled the piece of meat out of his mouth and recoiled when he saw a paperclip lodged inside it. He started cutting up everything he had cooked and found paperclip after paperclip hidden in his food. Throwing it all into the fire, he rushed away from the scene. He stood still, his eyes staring into the emptiness of the distance around him. Gathering courage, he approached the fire slowly, peeking into the sizzling mess he had made and saw there was not a single paperclip in sight.

*

Noah's eyes were wide open as sunrise graced the walls of his room. He had not slept at all, for his thoughts and fear of what had happened hadn't let him. He was also sure that he had heard the printer again during the night, only this time closer, just outside his bedroom door, but he had not been brave enough to look. He knew he had to see his grandmother again because Noah felt like this isolation was making him go insane. He had his coffee and bowl of porridge and then spent two hours picking redcurrants into large buckets. Once that was done, he made himself look somewhat decent, despite the violent, dark circles around his eyes.

An hour later, he was sitting at the wonky little table in his grandmother's kitchen. She was preparing cold beetroot soup, and although he had insisted that he could help, she had swatted him away.

'I know that look of yours, sweetie,' she said as she glanced at him for a brief moment while cutting up some strands of dill. 'You look preoccupied. Had the same expression when you were a child. What's wrong?'

He sighed heavily, 'I think I'm going crazy.'

'I'm not surprised. Our entire family has never been quite sane.'

'I'm seeing things that aren't there.'

'Now that's a step further than most of us have been,' she put down the knife and turned to face him, wiping her hands on her apron, tiny specks of dill getting stuck to the fabric. 'What have you been seeing?'

'Things to do with work.'

'Oh well, that's normal. You did escape the city because you were overworked.'

'But still, that's not good, is it?'

'Not really. But if you get it all out of your system, then maybe that's what you need to find some peace of mind.'

'Maybe,' Noah murmured and sighed.

'Don't look so glum. I did think that you living in that house alone might not do you any good. You should find a nice girl to keep you company.'

'I don't think that would help.'

'Noah, we all need someone.' She paused and then smiled. 'I know that I live here with just Artemis, but that's because I gave that whole thing a chance, and after three divorces, you really can't be arsed to find someone else. You haven't even had one, so that already works in your favour.'

'I did find a girl.'

'Oh?' She returned to chopping as if immediately understanding that Noah would find it easier to talk about his worries if she were not staring at him.

'I was dying in that job, just never stopping, and she made me stop for a second. Lizzie. I still don't know if I loved her or if I just loved the idea of her.'

'Why did she end things?'

'She didn't. I did.'

'Men,' she shook her head and tutted. 'Why would you do that if she helped you in that way?'

'I still don't know. Maybe that's what's haunting me. I can't really understand how I came to feel that I should give up on it. I just remember what I said to her when I did. I told her that I wish I could let her see how empty I feel. How this has been a pattern for me for years where nothing changes and that, with my fears and anxieties, I didn't know how to be someone's someone since I felt like I'm still struggling to be there for myself. I told her that I felt like I burdened her with my presence, and although she denied it, I know that she deserves someone better.'

'Those are strong words, dear, and I'm worried that you actually think they're true.'

'They are. I often feel so lost and restless, it's like I'm not really living, just doing enough to stay alive.'

'I think that everyone feels that to some extent.'

'Are you afraid of death, grandma?'

'Really? I thought your mother brought you up better than that. To ask an old woman if she's afraid of dying! The nerve!' She laughed heartily. 'But no, not really. When it comes to living, I feel like I've lived a life with no regrets. Maybe only marrying your grandfather. To fall in love with a man who I took care of as a nurse in the hospital when he was brought in because he had drunk too much and had driven his motorcycle into a ditch! What was I thinking? But I can live with that mistake, because everything else that came with it was worth it.'

'I'm constantly thinking about death. I know that it will happen, but I am so afraid of it that every time the thought crosses my mind, I feel panic overtake me, and pain in my chest.'

His grandmother walked over to him and touched his forehead with her rough palm, 'You're burning up, sweetie,' she opened a nearby cupboard and took out a bottle of Stolichnaya and a tiny shot glass. 'Have some of this.'

He shook his head, 'No, thank you.'

'Honestly, don't be stupid, Noah. You can have one drink, it won't kill you. Might do the opposite and actually make you feel like you're alive, for once. Also, you're not alone in having that fear. There's even a word for it, though I can't remember it just now.'

'Thanatophobia.'

He felt the liquid burn on its way down his throat and warm up his insides.

'I'll just say this, at least you're afraid of throwing your life away in theory, unlike many others in our family line. Although, indeed, it doesn't sound like you're really living it either. My mother tried to drown herself in a river because of unrequited love, and her mother tried to hang herself when she was young too. Both failed in their attempts, and I can assure you that they learnt how to appreciate life afterwards. So, like I said, at least you have some common sense in you. But I don't know what else to say other than that. People live for too long nowadays, that's why you have time to stop and think about death. We know that it's unlikely to be dramatic and that it's just waiting in the wings, so we almost wait for it too. A mutual attraction but an utterly toxic one. Your romance with Lizzie sounds much more appealing than this love affair you have going on with death.'

'Grandma, don't. This was a while ago. There's no point in

going back there again.'

'Then go forward somewhere!' she raised her voice. 'I'm sure you can get something from that will to live. Do you think that maybe your visions or whatever you've been going through is a sign that you should go back to the city?'

'Maybe,' Noah said, still unsure, but he felt as though deep down he had already made his decision. Her manner of scolding him had always helped him achieve the things that he wanted, which is why he knew that he had to talk to her about this too. His long-standing secret. He helped his grandmother set up the table, and they ate their lunch in silence, each contemplating their mortality in their own way.

*

Nothing had changed, yet again. However, Noah knew that he couldn't stay there any more. His mind did not yearn for peace, and this house was meant only for that. Locking the door, he closed his eyes and rested his forehead against the cherry-wood. It was a hot summer's day, and he could feel the sweat dripping down his neck. The same eternal stillness surrounded him, and although he was sorry to give it up, he knew that he didn't belong here. He would give it another shot. He would try to give living life another chance. Before he had said goodbye to his grandmother, she had mentioned Lizzie to him again, saying, 'I don't know anything about her, but Lizzie. Just from the name alone, that sounds like a nice person. From what you told me that you said to her, she really meant something to you. Maybe your happiness is there after all.' He had kissed her cheek and remained silent, but he knew that wasn't true. Noah had briefly fallen for her because of what she represented. Despite her own melancholy and anxieties, Lizzie was someone who truly lived and did not care whether she would wake up the next day. It was that which had drawn him to her like a moth to light, and when he realised that he could not steal just a bit of that mindset from her, he knew that it was not worth pursuing. Noah was sure that he would not look her up. Rather he would try to find someone who could teach him how to do this for himself. As his grandmother had said, the potential was there, and he still had just enough years ahead of him in order to have time to learn how to live. All the same, he had already booked a doctor's appointment.

The Clothes I Never Wear

It was one of those mornings when one can see their breath in the air as the autumn slowly becomes winter. Kathy was leaning against the bus stop wall, hands in her coat pockets, eyes bloodshot from both the early hour and the fact that she had drunk two bottles of wine the night before. Her lack of self-control and being unable to anticipate how miserable she would feel the next day always baffled her. This happened quite frequently.

I need to change, she thought to herself, her mind and body shivering from a lack of sleep and the cold wind blowing right through her.

The bus turned the corner and Kathy was soon on her way to the university. What followed was a day of seminars, and when it was over, and she was back in her bed, only then could she relax. She began her daily ritual of browsing through news sites, and amongst all the natural disasters and concerning political events, there was an opinion piece that caught her eye. The author was a woman who looked so effortlessly beautiful that Kathy immediately felt a pang of envy rushing through her. The article itself was an in-depth piece on this woman's lifestyle, which consisted of minimalism and natural and healthy living. Despite this being the complete opposite of Kathy's life, something about it appealed to her, and she began to read other articles written by the same woman. Engrossed in this process, she was suddenly brought back to reality by the sound of her phone ringing. It was Ian.

'Pick you up in half an hour?'

Kathy agreed, and the moment the call ended, she got ready. As she saw Ian's car pull up next to her apartment building, she felt glad that she had spruced herself up by taking a shower and touching up her make-up. She walked towards the car, trying to contain her smile. When she got in, he looked her over and said;

'I love the coat. Oh my god. Where did you get it?'

'I don't know, can't remember.' It was a dark leopard coat.

'I need to try it on,' Kathy laughed, but soon realised he was serious. 'Come on,' Ian got out of the car, which prompted her to do the same. She took it off and handed it over. Ian put it on, showing off and twirling around, clearly thinking that it suited him better. And it was true, it did. The coat was flashy and slightly out there, which matched his personality more than it did Kathy's. However, what was even more evident was that these insignificant spontaneous outbursts made Kathy jealous because she wished she could be like that. They got back into the car.

'So, where are you taking me tonight?' Kathy asked.

'We're going to start off with the beach. I've brought things to make a bonfire. And then I thought we might go for a stroll in a cemetery.'

'Sounds like a great plan.'

'I thought you'd like it.'

This was a routine of theirs. They were not in a relationship but saw each other every week, and when they did, it was always for a night drive followed by them spending the night together. As much as it pained Kathy that he could not commit to her, these adventures were something that she knew she could never voluntarily give up. Some time ago, she had given up on love because she had realised that in trying to escape from the pain of being her, she only ever found people who mirrored her own feelings about herself. Therefore, she knew that thinking that love would stop the pain and the fear was not the solution. Yet Kathy also knew that what she felt for Ian was as close to love as possible and it terrified her.

After a short drive, they arrived at the beach and made a fire, hiding from the wind between some dunes.

'What's one interesting thing you found out today?' Ian asked as he put his arm around her, cosying up to her side.

'It's not so much that I found out about it today, but rather I had some thoughts.'

'Tell me.'

'I thought about the people in my life and their personalities since I was trying to analyse mine.'

'And what conclusions did you come to?'

'I remembered this one moment, where I was having lunch with my parents and we all had watermelon for dessert.'

'Already a promising start.'

'So my dad took one of the pieces with the skin still on and, once he finished it, every last pink bit was scraped off. Then I looked at my mum's piece, and she had taken these haphazard bites from it, still leaving pink bits on it. While I had taken a knife and cut all of the fruit parts off perfectly and neatly. And I remember thinking how fascinating it is that you can see all of our personalities in this insignificant thing that we did. That these signs are everywhere, and as much as you can try to be someone else, you can't ever escape these give-aways.'

'How so? Are you telling me that you're trying to pretend to be someone you're not?' He nudged her playfully, although this was not a joke because this was precisely what he thought.

'Not exactly, but when it comes to our personalities, it's just so clear-cut. He's incredibly stingy with money and always wants to get the utmost from things, my mum is just a chaotic person in general, and me, well, I'm just a pedantic perfectionist, as you know. Ironic, isn't it, since the one thing that I can't perfect is myself?'

'You know that I don't think that you need to perfect anything. And that I hate it when you talk about yourself that way. What brought these thoughts to the surface?'

'Nothing really, it just came to me randomly.' She did not want to tell the entire truth. In fact, amongst other memories, this had been running through her mind as she was looking up the minimalist lifestyle since she knew that she was on the verge of yet another attempt to change her life. Her attempts were always superficial since they had to do more with her aesthetic, as she often decided to embrace either a certain decade in terms of her wardrobe or dress like a specific character she liked from a film. Kathy hoped that by doing this, the vibrant personalities of the people who lived in those decades or had been so alive on-screen would rub off on her. However, even though she was fully aware of how these changes came about, she was still not quite conscious that they never truly worked, despite the thought being at the back of her mind at every single try.

'And this is why I like to spend time with you. Because things like this just come to you,' Ian said.

Kathy smiled, but the hurt was still eating away at her because not too long ago, he had told her that the reason why they could never work was that her emotions were too flat, that she wasn't truly herself. Saying something like this would be enough for some people to understand that it should end there. Still, even though this was especially painful for Kathy, who already felt insecure about her personality, she could not let go of someone she had become so attached to. Especially, because he was everything that she wanted to be. Honest, full of life and, most importantly, unapologetically himself.

The fire soon turned into coals as they continued talking about Ian's day, leaving this topic behind, which pleased Kathy. He kissed her in between their conversation, which made her cheeks blush each time, but she was glad that he couldn't see it in the dim light of the glistening coal. Even though they had been seeing each other this way for months, he still made every single night feel like the first time they saw each other. He was good at creating the impression of making an effort.

Once they both started to feel too cold, they got into the car and drove back to Kathy's apartment, abandoning the cemetery plan. The moment they were underneath her floral sheets, the conversation seemed to slowly die out and turn into long looks. Soon their arms were wrapped around each other and they forgot their troubles, if only for a moment. Unfortunately, even when they were making love, Kathy's mind was always there, always pestering her and making her think of things that she would rather not be thinking of even during other more unremarkable moments. As Ian held her, Kathy thought about how unfair it was that he meant so much to her and that he was the only person she wanted, while she was certain that he would be fine with just about anyone. Yet, she would never be able to tell him that this was how she felt.

The room's darkness was suddenly disturbed by the small spark of a lighter as she lit her cigarette.

'What is one thing that you don't want to tell me but you feel like you should say?' Kathy asked, unsure why this question came with such ease.

'You make me feel inferior when I'm around you,' he said after giving it some thought. 'I don't feel interesting enough around you, but at the same time, this is only based on what goes on inside that head of yours, which I can only catch glimpses of. I just want to shout at you sometimes so that you would let it out, but even then, I don't think you would.'

He held his hand on her chest as she smoked as if trying to heal her lungs while the poison enveloped them. She didn't know what to say to that because too many thoughts immediately rushed to the surface of her mind, so instead she said nothing, knowing full well that this was exactly what irritated him. However, Kathy did know that she was beyond happy that she had this crazy and exciting soul next to her, despite it only ever being for brief moments. She put out her cigarette and lay down next to him, placing her arms around him and closing her eyes, feeling his breathing slow down next to her as he went to sleep.

*

Saturdays were not really Saturdays for a university student. Kathy began her day with multiple cups of coffee and doing the reading for her seminars the following week. However, once that was out of the way, it was time to change her life. She started by going to the store and buying groceries for the week. Once she got to the till her basket was full of vegetables, sparkling flavoured water with no sugar and no additives, an array of organic and paraben-free skincare, and a bottle of wine, which she could not do without, but at least that was marked as organic as well. Putting all these things away in her fridge and her cupboards at home, she tried not to think of the amount of money she had just spent but rather tried to embrace her new healthy lifestyle. She had also gone into some clothing stores and bought some very basic, mostly black and white pieces, whether it was a top or a skirt, which were on the more expensive side but sustainably made. Kathy then proceeded to clear out her wardrobe since she was determined to have only a few things in there and donate the rest.

Yet, as she had taken everything off the hangers and began going through the pile of clothes that lay upon her bed, it started to look more like a pile of memories. The most prominent part was her eighties-style blouses, all a different colour with gaudy, shiny buttons and shoulder pads. This had been her last phase, inspired by the New Romantics, which she had abandoned when she felt like she attracted too much attention. The leopard coat was just one remnant of that which she could still wear. Then there were the shades of brown and floral prints left over from her artistic phase, which had experienced an even shorter life-span. The most upsetting thing in her wardrobe was the one nineteen-sixties style dress that she found since this reminded her of the brief moment when she had ordered about ten such dresses online after watching Federico Fellini's film *8 ½*, yet she had only received the one since she had purchased them on a dubious site. When they never sent the rest, Kathy was already over her phase and couldn't be bothered with pursuing the matter further. Needless to say, these phases of hers often made her lose a lot of money. On and on it went until she realised that laid out before her were all her attempts to have a new life, her attempts to create a new her.

But this time will be different, she told herself out loud. *It has to be.*

These clothes went into one giant plastic bag and were put out of sight, as she had no desire to leave the house for a second time that day to donate them. She also cleared away any knick-knacks from the surfaces in her apartment so that everything would look clean and uncluttered.

After what she deemed to be a productive day, Kathy sat down by her windowsill, poured herself a glass of organic wine and then rolled a cigarette. Now that this was done, there seemed to be nothing left to do. Her one good friend was still out of town, visiting her fiancé, and Ian would be busy with work all day. As she sat and contemplated her day, she remembered a scene that stuck out to her in the grocery store, which she had not had time to reflect on while she was still there. When she was browsing the gluten-free food aisle, she had come upon an arguing couple. She was not quite sure what they were arguing about, but suddenly the girl had picked up a box of animal-shaped pasta, and with that, they had reconciled and began laughing over the goofy shapes, although the two were still visibly upset. It had somehow struck her as relevant, but she didn't know why. She made a note of it in her diary because she hoped it might lead to some interesting thoughts sometime in the future.

Soon the glass of wine turned into two, then three, and after a few hours, a tipsy Kathy returned from the store with two more bottles of organic wine, already regretting her choice to choose such an expensive lifestyle. The sky faded to lilac and then black, and around eight o'clock in the evening, she received a call from Ian, telling her he would pick her up in an hour, so Kathy put on her new clothes and was soon out the door.

*

A mirror had never seemed to be an entirely positive object to Kathy, but now it really did her no favours. Her eyes looked puffy, yesterday's mascara still gracing her dark circles, but more than that, her skin looked like an absolute disaster. Three weeks of using natural skincare had not had the magical and sublime effect that she had been promised, and so she felt more insecure than ever before. Her healthy diet had also done very little, as her constant drinking and smoking counteracted any of the possible benefits that she could gain from it. She returned to her flat from a day at university exhausted and hopeless since it always made her feel as though she was incompetent. But it had been made all the more devastating because she had gone to the bathroom in between classes and, seeing herself in the mirror, she had not recognised the broken and shabby person before her. Yet this gave her the determination to do what she should have already done weeks ago, which was to give up on this newest change. She threw away all of the new natural skincare and pulled out the bag of old clothes, which still sat at the back of the cupboard where she had hidden it. On her bus ride home, Kathy had decided to go back to whoever she was before. Even if it was something undefined, it was better than trying to fit in where she so clearly didn't belong. Yet with that came her revelation of just how absurd these phases of hers were. She had already taken notice of it when the pile that consisted of her lives was before her, but the denial to acknowledge it and the desire to change something had been too strong. However, she loathed the thought that she had been weak enough to now become susceptible to a movement which was largely aimed at people who were seeking such a change because of the unhappiness within themselves. It made her feel exploited and pathetic.

It is as if she was constantly trying to break the mould that was her true character, shaped throughout the years, but whatever she tried did not seem to work and instead, made her lose herself a little more each time. Perhaps these phases were her pasta animals. Nothing more than a temporary fix to make her feel better. Then a thought struck her. She had noticed that despite being so critical of everything she did, she would often catch herself saying 'I love you' out loud or in her head during the most mundane moments, and every time she did, she never really understood whether she was saying this to herself or about someone in her life since the thought was never associated with anything in particular. However, in this moment, she realised this was significant. It told her that something inside of her was telling her that, whoever she was, she felt something. Kathy realised that feeling outweighed everything she had used to conceal herself from the world.

The Regal Chair and the Student

The trees ruffled violently as they made their way to the apartment. Their hair covered their faces, and the wind blew up their coats. It was a dark and stormy afternoon, which would soon give way to the calm of the evening when the sky would turn to warmer colours as it said its goodbye.

The apartment was overcrowded, resembling a kindergarten, as everyone was curled up on the floor, waiting with their plates for the cake to be served. This was an awkward gathering initially presented as something entirely different. It was sold to them as a gathering of artists, but only a few of them were there, one of them being the host herself. The couple couldn't help from smiling at the long silences when everyone was racking their brain to find a clever thing to throw into the mix of unsuccessful conversation topics.

The girl was stunning in her charm and grace, her freshly coloured tangerine hair catching the few remaining sun's rays. The man by her side took large gulps of his beer, looking sleepy and unimpressed. His style was somewhere between punk and new wave, while hers could only be described as very sleek and minimalistic. They sat huddled close together, isolating themselves, but she did not cease to whisper to him about her desire to speak to the nice people who were present. He didn't seem to share her enthusiasm. They soothed their embarrassed nerves with alcohol and so in only a few hours they, along with everyone else, were no longer afraid of one another. People moved around and about, changing their little cliques rapidly in order to preserve these talks, so that they could later label them brief encounters. Soon the living room, which had been so very lively, was deserted but for the trio which stayed behind. Ivy, the girl who was hosting the evening and the man sat on a sofa, while Louise took a seat in an old, rococo style, cherry wood armchair with a floral, dusty pink satin fabric covering.

As she sat down, jittery from the liquor and excitement, her eyes took on a dazed look. It became clear that something was trying to escape her heart. She cast a serious glance at Ivy, raising her left eyebrow, which made her look just like an Eastern European Vivian Leigh, and spoke, 'Ivy, I'd like to propose a business transaction. Name anything that I could do so that you would give me this chair.'

Ivy sighed and gave a little laugh, her eyes slightly closed with sleep.

'I'm not going to give you the chair, Louise.'

'What? Why?' Suddenly alert, she leaned forward. 'You're moving out in two days anyway, and you said you're not taking any furniture with you.'

'You know that I willingly give away my things, the ones I don't need, but I just realise that it would be Matt who would have to get it to your place somehow.' At this, the man stopped sipping his beer and joined in firmly:

'Lou, you don't need that chair. There is no way we'd be able to get it into a taxi and I'm not going to carry it across town. It doesn't go with the look of your place.'

'I'll carry it myself. Ivy, what do you want for it?'

'Nothing. I'd give it to you for free, but it's a silly idea. Matt will have to carry it, and then what will you do with it afterwards when you have to move?'

Louise stroked the armrests and sighed angrily. Meanwhile, the kitchen and other rooms buzzed with people, and once in a while, a lonely wanderer came into the living room to grab a dumpling or a potato pancake, oblivious to the tension which permeated the air.

'But I really want it!' Louise suddenly exclaimed, unable to stop the passion from spilling out from her.

The two befuddled souls on the sofa looked at each other and laughed. This exchange between them was not malicious but rather kind as they were both used to Louise's occasionally entertaining outbursts.

'Louise, if you can pick up that chair and carry it to the door of the living room, then we can take it,' Matt said.

Her eyes widened in horror. 'Are you serious? You want me to pick up this chair?'

'Yes, and carry it.'

'Do you want to embarrass me somehow?'

'In front of who? There is no one here except us.'

Louise stood up determined, granted a couple of minutes after this exchange had taken place, and walked behind the chair. She carefully removed the mustard coloured quilt placed on the back of the chair as if it added extra weight, prompting a laugh from both Ivy and Matt. Then with the most composed expression she could muster, she grabbed the armrests, hugging the large piece of furniture, and lifted it off the ground. Only for a moment, and then it fell right back onto the tribal carpet.

'So, we're not taking it,' Matt laughed and rose to go to the window with a cigarette between his teeth. As he walked, Ivy cast a glance of pity at the slight limp in his right leg. Once he reached the window, he stood there quietly when he caught Louise's gaze. Aimed at him, it was furious, unforgiving and petrifying. Finally, unable to withstand this silence, Ivy spoke:

'Lou, it's best if you forget about it. In the end, the things you own end up owning you. Look at me, I've hoarded a room full of items I don't need and can't bring with me, only because they were cheap or I found them on the street, like this chair. You don't think about how impractical it is at the time, but I'm telling you that you will regret it.'

Louise pursed her scarlet lips into a pout, her eyes beginning to water, but this was not perceptible to the others. Then Matt walked over to her and picked up the chair. The strain of its weight could be seen on his features. He put it down.

'I'm not carrying this.'

The party took place in the other rooms while the living room had become a war zone. The chair now seemed as valuable as gold.

'Ivy, this is, after all, a business transaction. What do you want for the chair?'

'Nothing,' Ivy sighed, exhausted. 'That's not the point.'

'I can have it then?'

'Of course, you can have it. I just don't know how you will…'

A loud squeal of ecstasy came from Louise as she rushed to sit back down on her treasure. Her eyes glittered with untainted happiness. It was the happiest anyone had seen her in months.

'I'm not carrying it,' Matt muttered again.

'I don't care. I love it so much that I'll do anything to get it back home.'

*

The following day, Matt carried the chair to Louise's apartment almost halfway across town. There, among Ikea furniture and modern appliances, it seemed out of place. The more one looks at Louise, the more one realises that the armchair does not suit her personality at all. It suits the type of person that she wants to be. The more one looks at Matt and Louise as a couple, the same is true of Matt. Nevertheless, the chair now stands in the corner of a different living room, on a different carpet, in a different person's possession. Louise loves it, at least for now. Months later, she will have to move out of the country, so she will have to decide if she will take it with her. Perhaps she will, or by that time, Louise might already have forgotten why she liked it so much, and it will end up back on the street, however, this is unlikely. Items or people that represent something that we aspire to be are the ones we want the most and also the ones which are the hardest to part with. What Louise does not understand, however, is that because of this, she now possesses something that owns her.

People Are People

'I can't believe we've already been sitting here for an hour,' Remy sighed.

A long line of cars stretched out ahead of them with no reason for the traffic jam in sight.

'Driving takes patience. But you're doing really well. Keeping a good distance from the car in front of you,' Alfie smiled as if understanding her frustration, yet there was something in his demeanour that gave away that he was not in the least bit bothered by their predicament.

'It seems fascinating to me that, as a driving instructor, you must spend so many hours of your life stuck in traffic jams. I feel like there's a metaphor in there somewhere just waiting to be made, you know, something along the lines of wasting your life away.'

'It's usually very easy if you're not stuck in a car with someone who is telling you that you're wasting your life,' he laughed, and it warmed Remy's heart. She loved the fact that she could say whatever came into her mind and he would always take it as banter and joke with her about it.

'What are your plans for the weekend?' she asked, with her next question already in mind.

'Nothing that exciting. I'll probably try to drive out to the seaside, go for a walk, meet up with some friends. What about you?'

'I'm going to a festival this weekend. Something very artsy

and alternative, whatever those things mean. That's what my friends told me about it anyway,' Remy shrugged and then felt that little rush of anxiousness just as she was about to ask him if maybe he would like to join her. She knew there were still tickets left. She had checked.

'Oh, so lots of drinking and people off their heads on drugs, huh?'

'Probably. I'm aiming to not be one of them. Although the drinking will most definitely happen.'

'I used to be into all of that. I went through a very rough time in my late teens and early twenties, and I thought that alcohol was my problem solver. I was so wrong about that. Because once I stopped, I realised that for the most part, it had actually been the source of all of those problems.'

'You don't drink at all now?'

'No, alcohol-free for nine years now.'

'Wow. So what have you replaced that with?'

'People. A supportive community. Nature. Music. There are other things out there, Remy.'

'Thanks for enlightening me,' she laughed and then drove the car forward slightly.

'You're very welcome. Seriously though, I'm not trying to be patronising, just helpful. My friends and I are actually going to be part of this event tomorrow afternoon, which is like a community thing; you could come along and see if it's your kind of thing.'

'What kind of event?'

'Outdoor concerts, a food market, some talks being given by a couple of smart people. It's taking place in Queen's park.'

'Ooh, that actually sounds nice. I might have to stop by.'

'Please do. It's free, and everyone is welcome.'

'I think I'll take you up on your offer. Not like I have much to do tomorrow anyway,' Remy thought she'd crash into the car in front of her. It felt like fate. Just as she was about to invite him out, he had stepped up and done it for her.

*

Christina was waiting for her next to a kiosk. Remy admired her from a distance. Not only was Christina beautiful, but she was incredibly good at being an adult. Even now she was on the phone, fixing a problem at work, while looking beyond effortless. She had maintained a steady job as an editor at a magazine for four years already. She was in a happy relationship and every time they met, she was full of stories she had heard on her favourite podcasts. Remy was far from that. She was working in a supermarket during the summer holidays and was still awaiting her final year of university as she hadn't been able to decide what to study for far too long. What scared her the most was that she liked her job. She liked doing the same thing over and over again, which in her case mostly consisted of checking the expiry dates of the produce and moving things around on shelves. Remy knew that she would be genuinely satisfied with working in that store for years or in a similar job that required the same type of repetitive activities, such as working in the sorting room of a post office, but her parents would never approve, and she also knew that she did want to earn more than she was earning right now.

'Tell me where we're going because you've been so mysterious about this whole thing,' Christina said as she gave her a smooch on her cheek.

'I told you, I don't even know. I just know that we need to go there because this is my chance with Alfie.'

'And what will I do there?'

'Be my wing woman. Or just wander around the food market,' she laughed.

Christina rolled her eyes. 'The things I do for you.'

They headed in the direction of the park. The day was brightly lit, sunshine reflecting off the cars scorching in the heat. Remy regretted her choice of a black top as soon as she left the house, but at least she looked quite edgy with her leopard mini skirt, loafers and her lips painted scarlet red. She could see from a distance that there were quite a lot of people wandering around the park, which in her mind was a good thing since Christina would have more to do. As they walked through the park gate, they were greeted by two women handing out brochures, which the pair of them happily accepted, although Remy felt like the women gave her strange looks. Always one to do so, she immediately stuffed the brochure into her bag and started to look through the crowd to see if she could spot Alfie. Christina, on the other hand, read through it attentively.

'Um, Rems, I didn't know this was a Christian thing.'

'What?' She gasped.

'This is an event organised by one of the local church groups. It says so right here.' She pointed to the piece of paper.

'I didn't know that Alfie was religious,' Remy said.

'Well, we're certainly not. There's some interesting info here, talks a lot about there only being one love for each of us but not before Jesus, of course. They are also really trying to reinforce the point that this is a great opportunity for those who are lost to find the true meaning in life.'

'I think I definitely look lost,' Remy said, as she realised that her outfit made her stand out from the crowd like a bright pink flamingo among penguins.

'Do you still want to stay?'

'Well, I'd at least like to say hi to Alfie, but I don't think we should stay for too long. I feel like we're crashing someone's party.'

'Yeah, that's one way to put it.'

They walked along the park's winding paths, past the stages where a variety of things were taking place. On one of them, a priest gave a speech about the importance of values and tradition, which did feel very politicised and racist as he mentioned 'the others' several times. On another stage, people were gathered in a group that resembled an AA meeting, and it appeared that this was exactly what they were doing; talking about their burdens and struggles. Christina and Remy stopped at a different stage because it seemed too intriguing to pass up since it was announced that there would be a Christian hip-hop band performing. As the performance started, Remy noticed Alfie only a short distance away with a group of people. His blond hair was swept back, he was standing tall, and he looked more handsome than ever in his white button-down shirt and light-coloured jeans. Remy pinched Christina on the arm, and nodded in his direction. Christina gave a nod of approval, and with that, Remy began to move through the sparse crowd towards him.

'Hey hey,' she said as she placed her hand on his back to make him notice her.

'Remy, you came! I'm so glad.' He turned towards her and seemed to create a barricade between her and the group of people he had been with. 'How are you finding it so far? Isn't the atmosphere just great?'

'Yeah, everyone seems lovely. I didn't know this was a religious event, though.'

'It's not like I was hiding that from you. It's just that it's not even about that. It's about community, bringing people together,' his tone seemed defensive, so Remy decided not to pursue this conversation any further.

'Would you be willing to show me around?' She gave him a coy smile, and he responded in turn.

'Sure. What's your preference – music, food or conversations?'

'Food, probably. I need to pick up my friend, though. I left her by the stage over there.'

'Great, let's do that first then.'

They walked over to where Christina was standing, her brow furrowed as if she was vigorously pondering the meaning behind the lyrics of the hip-hop songs. Remy introduced her to Alfie, and she could see that Christina immediately understood why Remy had taken a liking to him. It was difficult not to. They left the stage and wandered over to a food market where every single seller seemed almost overbearingly nice. Remy bought herself a sandwich and an iced tea to quench her thirst, but what she really wanted was a glass of something stronger for her nerves, however, there was no alcohol in sight. What followed was an hour of small talk as the three of them sat down at a picnic table. It was mostly Alfie and Christina just getting to know each other, which left little for Remy to say. Despite that, she felt like the day was already a success, and when an hour later Alfie excused himself because he had to go and talk to some of the people from his church group. Remy did not mind and just light-heartedly said, 'We'll probably be going soon, but I'll see you at the next driving lesson!' He nodded and gave her one of his disarming smirks.

'As handsome as that boy is, don't let him drag you into something that doesn't match who you are,' Christina added as she saw Remy melting before her.

'I won't. Although it's not like this is some sort of cult. It's just good old fashioned religion.'

'Yes, but you've never been religious, so why start now?'

'That feels a bit cynical. I'm open to new ideas.'

'They have very old ideas.'

'You know what I mean.'

'Just… be careful,' Christina sighed and watched Remy's eyes follow Alfie as he walked away.

*

'It looks like someone stayed up until three o'clock in the morning again,' Will grinned as he sipped his coffee behind the counter, watching Remy.

'I may have, yes.'

'What were you reading?'

'I had to finish "Girl, Woman, Other,"' she sighed, putting on her name tag.

'Ooh, tell me! What did you think?'

'I mean, it was incredible. I don't remember the last time I was that sucked into a story.'

'Right? The writing was b-e-a-u-t-i-f-u-l,' his hand gestures almost made his coffee cup spill over. 'I feel like I want to read it again even though I only read it three weeks ago.'

'Hello, hello,' Daisy said pleasantly as she walked through the door.

'Morning! Guess who had another late night?' Will smirked.

'Remy, why do you do this to yourself?' she teased.

'I don't know. I just know that I need coffee,' Remy mumbled as she put the kettle on.

'Was it a good book at least?'

'The best.'

'I admire your dedication to reading, though. I am working through my pile of books that I want to read very slowly. I feel like I was better at reading books in school than I am now, as paradoxical as that may be. I feel like I need someone to tell me "you need to read this book by this specific date and analyse it!"'

'We can do it for you!' Will immediately jumped at the opportunity.

'I might find that a bit patronising,' Daisy laughed. 'What about starting a book club? That'd give me plenty of incentive.'

'Oh, I'd totally be up for that!' Will said without even giving it much thought.

Remy paused before saying, 'Maybe that could be fun.' However, she wanted to say a resounding 'no', yet she wasn't good at saying that to her friends.

'Great! I could make a list of all the books I want to read, and you two could do the same and then we could switch between our lists every week or so?'

'*Hmm*, I suppose that could work,' Remy didn't care much for this conversation.

'Okay, I'll do that once I get home. Have to warn you though, my list will be around a hundred books long,' Will said.

'Well, hopefully, we stay friends long enough to go through all of them in our little book club! I'll start coming up with names for the club this evening!' Daisy was so excited that Remy felt as though she would clap her hands with joy at any moment.

'Cool! What a productive morning!' Will said as he was heading off into the direction of the stock room. 'Back to work now, fellow book nerds!'

Later that evening, as Remy was chopping up carrots for her

favourite vegetable soup recipe, her phone started pinging non-stop from an endless number of incoming messages. Daisy had created a new group chat for the three of them and was already sending over her list of books she wanted the book club to read. Will was eagerly egging her on, commenting on nearly every one of her choices. Remy took a quick look at the messages and then turned her phone on silent and placed it face down on her kitchen counter. She returned to making dinner, however, her mood was ruined. What frustrated her the most was that she had this inability to say no. This was not the first time it affected her life, but somehow it felt like the last straw. She knew that she should have said no to the book club idea immediately because now it already felt like it was too late. If she were to back out now, it would feel rude since three people for a book club was already pushing it, but two were simply not enough, and both Daisy and Will seemed so excited about it.

It bothered her that it seemed like people constantly felt the need to reduce their interests from something private to them to a group activity. She loved talking to Daisy and Will about the books that she was reading, and she loved hearing them talk about the ones they had read, however, their tastes in books were so vastly different. Daisy loved historical fiction and biographies, Will was a fan of science fiction and young adult novels, while Remy loved both the classics and contemporary romance novels. Their interests did not match, and so she knew that with this book club, she would be forced to read books that she often found uninteresting or ones that dealt with topics that she could not relate to. Although the thought of exposing yourself to new ideas had always appealed to her, she did not want it to become a part of her routine and akin to something that was out of her control, just another chore that she had to do. However, she came back to the conclusion that it was already too late to back out. She stared at her pile of unread books, the colourful spines glistening marvellously next to her velvet armchair, and sighed.

*

The pub was one of her small pleasures. Cheap and greasy food, beer in sticky pint glasses, the hum of people all telling their stories simultaneously to their friends, the honey glow of the afternoon sun gracing them during after work drinks. She felt at home there. Christina sat down at their table after returning from the bathroom. Remy could see that she had touched up her lipstick and applied some powder. Christina always looked put together and constantly strived to maintain that image, even in the casual atmosphere of a local pub.

'This is exactly what I need right now,' she said after taking a big sip of her fresh pint.

'Same, it's been a stressful couple of days,' Remy added.

'What's been going on? Is it your driving instructor? Remind me of his name again.'

'Alfie, and no, that's very much over. I have my last lesson with him next week, but I cannot wait to get it over with. We're just really not compatible.'

'What? When did this happen? I could see pink cartoon hearts in your eyes when you were looking at him just two weeks ago. I mean I am so relieved. The Jesus thing was a bit too much.'

'True, although he is a really good guy. I've constantly been attracted to such jerks, so it felt refreshing to like someone unproblematic. However, the more I thought about it, the more I realised how quickly I'd grow bored.'

'Exactly. As much as I hate to say it, you need someone

who's a bit of a wild card.'

'*Ugh*, I hate that that's true. I'm doomed to have complicated relationships for the rest of my life.'

'Now that's a bit too dramatic,' Christina laughed and raised her glass. 'Cheers!'

'Sure, why not cheer to that?' Remy rolled her eyes, 'Actually, I've had a couple of thoughts this past week, and I feel like I should tell someone about it because they've been nagging at me. I think that's why I decided to let go of Alfie.'

'Go ahead.'

'So Alfie, right, he's in that church group with all those people, and they are his friends, but I thought, what do they really have in common other than religion? This thing happened to me last week where I was forced into a book club by my work colleagues, Daisy and Will. I think you've met them once or twice. I say forced because I couldn't say no, which is just so typical of me. But the more I thought about this book club, the more it reminded me of the church group.'

'How so?'

'It just seems to me that not all of those people in that church group may be compatible, even as friends, I mean. So they are all just forming this group around their love for Jesus and their religion, which is just one facet of their personalities. Like with the book club. Yes, I'm friends with Daisy and Will, but it's not just because we all like to read books. It just seems bizarre to me that people can't just be satisfied with forming friendships but rather that they have to form these specific groups instead.'

'I can kind of see where you're going with this. But to play devil's advocate here, why not do it?'

'Because I feel like whenever you limit something to this specific thing or interest and create a structure for it, that thing can start to feel more like a task rather than something that binds people together organically. Like I have no desire to be a part of this book club, with its deadlines and set reading list, so I feel like I may start to resent it over time, and I hate myself for even thinking that an activity which I am signing up to do with my friends may become something that I find burdensome. Same with the church group. There is no way I believe that every single person there is always up for going to their meetings or their events, but instead, I think that they feel like they have to do it out of a sense of obligation, a sense of duty.'

'To be fair, I feel like you're borrowing some ideas from anarchists there,' Christina laughed and nudged Remy.

'But you see what I'm getting at, right?'

'Oh, completely. I am proud to say that I have embraced this philosophy of yours for years, as I have not been part of any clubs or groups.'

'Well, I've tried to avoid it constantly as well. However, recent events have made me think about it a bit too much.'

'When are you going to tell Daisy and Will that you're not doing the book club?' Remy sighed and, avoiding Christina's eyes, continued to sip her drink.

*

The steering wheel was burning hot as the car had been sitting outside in the sun before their driving lesson. They turned on the air conditioning and sat for a moment, waiting for the car to cool down.

'Thanks again for coming to our event that time,' he smiled, almost shyly.

'It was sweet of you to invite me. I had a lot of fun.'

'I'm glad to hear that. If you want to, you can come along to our meeting this Saturday at St. Paul's church.'

Remy knew that she needed to clarify that this would never happen, but words failed her. Despite what she had said to Christina, her feelings for him were still very much there.

'I don't know if I'm interested in joining your church group, which is where I feel like this is going,' she tried to laugh it off as if implying that he was trying to get her to join a cult.

'I didn't think you were,' there was a hint of disappointment in his voice.

'But I would like to see you again outside of the confines of this Toyota. Would you like to go for a coffee sometime?'

'Remy, I'd like to, but I'm afraid I can't.'

'That's an interesting choice of words,' though she said it playfully, it was only to suppress the sting they'd caused.

'I mean, I can't date anyone outside of my church group, or rather my religion that is.'

'Oh.'

'I'm sorry. I do really like you. It just wouldn't work; it'd be too complicated.'

'Does it not bother you that you're limiting your pool of people to such a small number?'

'I've never thought about it that way. In fact, I feel like it makes things simpler because I know that the people I end up seeing will share my values.'

Remy did not know how to refute that and she understood that it would be pointless to argue about this matter any further. She did not know whether this reinforced the thoughts she had had over the last few days or caused them to fall apart. The day before, she had told Daisy and Will that she did not want to be a part of their book club as much as she liked discussing books with them. They had been visibly saddened by that and had decided to abandon the idea because it would be no fun to do it just between them. They did say that they would buddy read a couple of books because that would still provide a solution to the original problem, which was Daisy's recent lack of incentive to read. However, Remy had left work that day feeling as if she had let them down and worrying that they might feel deceived by her decision. Had this affected their friendship? Maybe not in the long run, but, as silly as it seemed, Remy knew that her choice would linger at the back of her mind for at least the next few weeks. Perhaps friendship means accepting the parts that don't match between you and your friends. To indulge their wishes, especially when there is a majority, and offer a small sacrifice in return for more time together and an even closer bond. Was this what Alfie had signed himself up for, she wondered. Could the reward of this tight community outweigh the differences that were there? Maybe some people were better at living this way, more selfless at least. Apparently, Remy was not.

The car had cooled down. She turned the key and waited for his instructions, wishing to wipe the slate clean.

The Missing Postcard

For Eve

Museums intimidated her so she never went to them. When travelling, Hazel preferred to walk around and look at the buildings, the parks, the daily life of those living in whichever city she visited. Art galleries full of contemporary paintings, in particular, filled her with dread because she didn't feel anything. The times she had been in one, Hazel merely spent a minute or so in front of each painting, staring at it blankly, wishing it would tell her how to feel. Therefore, it was so unlike her to go into one voluntarily. She had been walking around Stockholm in the early morning hours, cold wind sneaking under her coat and freezing her face, the snow underfoot making walking difficult, when she saw the nearly empty gallery and thought she could warm up and grab a coffee in the museum café. However, as she went in and saw the posters for the exhibition, she was drawn to it.

It was an exhibition of the paintings of Hilma Af Klint, a turn-of-the-century Swedish artist. More specifically, her series of giant almost floor to ceiling paintings called *De tio största* or *The Ten Largest*. The exhibition note stated that the artist had specified in her will that her work should be kept secret for at least twenty years after her death because she felt that people were not yet ready to receive the message it would contain. The note indicated that her art was intended to convey transcendental messages to those who view it, that her paintings offered a glimpse into the spiritual realm.

This time, as Hazel stood in front of the paintings, she did feel something. A powerful wave of serenity and almost sleepiness. The titles of the paintings led Hazel through a journey from *Childhood* to *Youth*, *Adulthood* and *Old Age*. The warm tones felt like a lullaby, the various abstract shapes non-threatening. The colours were calming; pastels, pinks, purples, a bit of orange and mustard yellow. Words received by the artist from the spirits appearing throughout. She wanted to be inside the paintings, especially the second in the series, one called *Childhood*, as the sea blue background felt like home. Hazel did not even realise that she had spent two hours there. The room had filled up. It no longer felt as intimate as it had before. She slowly moved away from the paintings, thinking how nice it would be to have at least one of them at home, covering one entire wall of her living room in her tiny flat in Glasgow. She went over to the museum shop and found a display of the postcards of the paintings. She took one of each and then came to realise that one was missing. There were ten paintings but only nine postcards. She turned to the shop assistant, a young girl with a smile that instantly made you love her. Hazel asked her if the tenth postcard could be purchased and the girl flashed her smile and simply said, 'No'. The lack of explanation made Hazel feel awkward so she didn't ask her again and just bought the cards she had already picked up.

Later that day, Hazel was passing her time in a restaurant at the airport. She had finished off a huge slice of lasagne, two glasses of wine and was now having cake and coffee. It was the first time in her life she was alone for her birthday. She thought how silly it was that she could have spent one more day in Stockholm and spent her birthday having dinner in a nice restaurant, maybe had a bubble bath in her hotel room, rather than waiting for a plane back home, but she had let the slight difference in ticket prices affect her decision. She was always too sensible and she hated herself for it. The postcards were poking out of her bag and so she had a look at them again. The one that wasn't there was important. Hazel knew it. Maybe the gallery had chosen not to sell all of them together because, given that they did have those secret messages from the spirits encoded within them, the ten of them together would simply be too powerful therefore it was risky to do so. Maybe she was completely exaggerating. Then she thought about the girl again and the way she had said, 'No', so decisively, as if there was no possible way that they would sell her the tenth postcard. Moreover, no other explanation made sense either. It was not as though absolutely everyone had wanted that postcard in particular and so it had been sold out – there hadn't even been a separate slot for it in the display at the shop. She didn't know why it was bothering her so much but it was on her mind the whole way home.

*

Hazel opened her eyes and was greeted with yet another cold and rainy day. She put on her fluffy dressing gown and went to the kitchen to make a cup of tea. She heard the drop of the mail at her front door but was in no rush to get it, knowing that it was bound to consist of bills and more bills. It was still dark outside, the rain visible against the glare of the streetlights. Morning traffic filled the street below and she sat on the armchair and stared at the people who were more productive than she was, those who went to work early. Suddenly, an intrusive thought entered her mind. She remembered that moment, from the day before, when she had returned to her empty flat, all quiet and cold, lacking love. Her cat Toffee was at a friend's place so she didn't even have him to keep her company. She had put her suitcase down and sat down beside it and cried for a while. Then she had got up, gone to make some tea, unpacked and enjoyed a cosy night in bed with a book, as though nothing had happened. Hazel knew she was good at living in denial and often wondered if it was unnatural – her being able to switch from mood to mood like that. Then again, no one else saw that side of her so it didn't really matter.

Finally, ready to face the world she got dressed while listening to the morning news and had a quick breakfast. As she was about to leave her flat she picked up the mail and glanced at it. Behind the envelopes containing her bills, she noticed the corner of something colourful. When she looked at what it was, she was unsure whether to be dramatic and drop it to the floor and scream, or if she was perhaps still dreaming and none of this was real. She put the bills on her entrance table but stuck the postcard in her bag before rushing out the door. As she sat on the train on her way to work, she resisted the urge to look inside her bag. She thought that surely there was absolutely no way it was in there and when she would check it at work, she'd realise that it was just her imagination.

At work her mind was elsewhere. Thoughts rushed in and she was forced to confront them. It was the first birthday she had spent alone and it just so happened to be her thirty-fifth. Hazel had not even realised it before, or maybe she had but merely subconsciously. She didn't want to think about her mum but now that she had made the connection, she couldn't escape it. She never understood and will never understand, which is why the hurt always lingered there at the edges of her mind. She was procrastinating now and she knew it. Just sorting her papers, writing to-do lists but none of it was actual work. She didn't want to think about her mum and she didn't want to check her bag. Lunch came and went. The day grew from dark to light to dark again, and Hazel was on her way back home.

After a dinner of store-bought pizza and some wine, she finally felt like she was ready. The one thing that had come of this was that Hazel realised that she really needed a smaller bag and to get rid of half the stuff that she carried around with her all the time because save for her phone and wallet – items which she mostly kept in her pockets anyway – she had not reached for anything else that was in there throughout the whole day. Once again, she was procrastinating and she scolded herself for it. Hazel took her bag into her lap and opened it. The card was still in there. It was a postcard of the painting titled *Childhood*, the one she had felt the most drawn to.

Two overlapping circles against a light blue background and above that was an array of circles, ovals and flowers of lighter, more gentle colours. It's as though the two overlapping circles were the focus and they felt heavy against everything else, like there was a sense of friction between them. A hint of something sinister. The rest of it reminded Hazel of summers, playgrounds, funfairs, a sense of joy. However, that is not what she felt in that moment. This had been the missing postcard and now it had ended up on her doorstep along with her mail. Hazel thought she must be going insane. Trying to rationalise everything, as she usually did, she tried to convince herself that she must have bought it at the museum shop, it must have been there and she must have placed it amongst her mail all by herself. Then again, she could not for the life of her understand why she would do such a thing. Maybe to have some drama, some mystery in her otherwise mundane life. She didn't know, but at that moment she did prefer the idea that she was just bonkers and not that some higher power had sent the card to her flat.

Hazel blue tacked all the postcards to her wall. They looked nice there but she was hoping that when she woke up the next day and went into her living room, there would only be nine of them there.

*

The morning announced itself with gusts of wind knocking the branches of a nearby overgrown tree against her bedroom window. She turned on the small lamp on her bedside table and stayed in bed for a few minutes, staring at the ceiling, letting the silence calm her. Reluctantly, she put on her dressing gown and went to the living room. As she turned on the light and cast a glance at the wall, she didn't even have to count them to know. It was clear that there were only nine. Hazel didn't know whether to feel relief or panic because she might be going crazy. Tea, first, she thought.

Her mother had loved her. She knew that much. Hazel remembered the lemony scent of her hair, the way it sometimes tickled Hazel's nose when she was curled up next to her and listened to her mother read a bedtime story. She would stop at times and kiss the top of Hazel's head, a small gesture but it showed that her mum simply could not contain the love she felt, she had to show it. Those were vague memories, becoming foggier by the year. She wasn't even sure what would be better; to know that her mother hated her, had never loved her, or that she had this love but chose to leave Hazel behind anyway.

She remembered what James told her when they had their

final talk, just three weeks ago. His words cutting her, seeping into every part of her that she had kept safe:

'You are so afraid to lose me that it's smothering. The pressure of knowing that if we become even more attached, build on this even more and then something happens and we have to end it, that I have to leave you, knowing that this would shatter you, makes me so afraid. I can't do this, I'm sorry.'

She had wanted to cling to him, not let go, exactly as he'd said but she held back and let him leave and it did shatter her. How clearly our past sets us on a path scattered with all the issues we already know we are bound to face. James had not been in touch since then, not even to wish her a happy birthday, which Hazel understood. It is easier to cut it off entirely, pretend it never happened in the first place.

She sipped her tea and looked at the postcards.

*

On her way back from work, Hazel popped into the Waterstones on Sauchiehall Street. Not only was she trying to escape the rain and looking for an excuse to buy more books, but also she actually had a legitimate reason for being there, as she wanted to find a gift for her best friend Daniel. He had also recently had his birthday and had celebrated it with his wife Izzy by going on a trip to Florence. A much better location than she had chosen for herself, Hazel thought, because at least they had been able to see some sun. Hazel browsed the shelves and found two books that she thought he might enjoy. She decided to sit down in the café as it was still raining heavily outside. She sunk into the leather armchair and enjoyed a decaf cappuccino. It felt safe there, as though being amongst people erased her thoughts.

She observed them, tried to ascertain their personalities, the relationships between them. It was nice to keep her mind busy this way. The waitress brought over the bill and Hazel wanted to pay immediately but as she lifted the receipt off the table she realised that it was not the only thing there. Underneath the receipt was the postcard again.

She called over the waitress, an older lady with the kind of cosy aura that adds to the feel of a place and, as she handed her the cash, Hazel blurted out, 'Sorry, did you bring this here with the receipt?' She slid the postcard towards her and tried to keep her hand from trembling.

'No, love. That must have been here already.'

'That's just the thing, it wasn't.'

'I don't know what to tell you, hun.' The waitress smiled, as if apologising. Hazel was not going to argue further, the lady was already being too nice. However, she hated the pattern that she was now noticing.

Hazel could not grasp what was happening. She did not want this, whatever it was. This felt like something that would happen to a main character in a film or a novel, but she had never wanted to be the main character. All she had ever wanted was an ordinary life. When she was little and her dad had given her near unlimited access to Cartoon Network because he didn't know what to do with her, how to make it better, Hazel's favourite show had been *Top Cat*. Not because of the storylines but simply because she enjoyed the credits scene so much. The cat winding down for the night, putting on his pyjamas, brushing his teeth and going to sleep. The simple routine of it all. She also liked that the cat was a bit of a jerk, already a bad sign for the future men she'd be interested in. However, whatever was happening to her now was so far removed from the life she had imagined for herself that she didn't know what to do with it.

Once the waitress left, she gathered up her things and fled, leaving the postcard behind.

Back at home, Hazel was obsessively Googling Hilma Af Klint. Not just the artist herself but she was trying to type in keywords that might lead her to stories of other people experiencing something similar to what she was going through but there was nothing. It felt like a message but Hazel was too afraid to wonder who it was from or what it was trying to convey. Just when she thought she had finally found a version of peace, her version of it, as flawed as it may be, this had torn it apart. She stared at the painting on Google again, trying to return to that calm feeling she had first felt when she had seen it back in Stockholm. However, this was in vain, as all she felt right now was severe anxiety. She stood up to head over to the kitchen to pour herself a strong glass of whiskey where she saw Toffee pawing at something under the pantry cupboard. Hazel picked up the chubby cat and bent down to retrieve the cat toy. She should have already known that it was not a toy. She pulled the postcard out from under the cupboard and immediately went over to her desk, took a pair of scissors and cut it up. She did not want to be silly and potentially anger any ghosts that were trying to communicate with her but she just didn't care for this. There was a line she had to draw so that the whole thing didn't become absurd.

'If you want to say something, just say it,' Hazel said this aloud and then went to pour herself that drink.

Maybe her mother would have been happy if she had never had a child. She could have just divorced Hazel's Dad and pretended that this chapter of her life had never happened. However, with Hazel's existence it meant that she couldn't do that. Hazel was a constant reminder. Then again, why would she have wanted to divorce him anyway? They had a quiet and comfortable relationship. She heard them argue once and even then it was over something so minor she couldn't even remember what it was. Why had her mother suffered? All those mornings when she took Hazel to kindergarten and seemed so thrilled to be by her side, to walk their little path through the park, rain or shine, it was difficult to acknowledge what had really been going on inside her mind. There must have been such a profound darkness there.

Hazel remembered that last day when her and her mum walked over to the kindergarten. It was one of those days that holds the promise of spring. The air feels warmer, the sun rays more encouraging, little flowers springing up from the grass. Her mum had seemed a bit more preoccupied that day but still had a smile on her face, especially when Hazel stopped to pick her flower. Before she could do that, her mum gently placed her hand on hers and told her to leave it to grow and become even more beautiful. Hazel had hugged her then because her mum looked so pretty in the sunshine. She was Hazel's light. When her day at kindergarten was over, her teacher told her that Hazel would have to stay there for a little while longer because her dad was on her way to pick her up. Hazel was confused and asked the teacher why her mum was not here and she could see that the teacher was sad but at that point she couldn't understand why.

*

The streets were calm, the Saturday shoppers had returned home, exhausted from their efforts, a mild afternoon sun was bouncing off the buildings in the city centre. Hazel was on her way to meet

Daniel. They were going out for drinks to celebrate their birthdays since, due to their trips, they were unable to do so before. She had known him since primary school. They became friends because they had no one else to be friends with. For Daniel it was because he was bullied by the other boys and for Hazel it was because she was so bad at interacting with people. They had to work on a project together for one of their classes and because of that she had discovered that they both loved reading. This was the one thing that opened her up and so she lost that fear with him that she had with everyone else. The fear that she would run out of things to talk about, that her mind would go blank and that whoever she was talking to would then ask about her mum and she would break down in tears.

They had seen each other through their best and worst times. Daniel had been there for her through James and Hazel had been there for Daniel with all of his other girlfriends and the heartbreak they left in their wake. This was before he met Izzy. She would trust him with her life and she knew he felt the same way. Although she wanted to enjoy the drinks that evening, Hazel knew that it would not be as simple as that. This was one final test, she thought to herself as she was making her way to the pub. There is that moment in almost every horror film when the character who is experiencing strange things has to tell their friends about it and, more often than not, the friends are dismissive and end up being proven wrong. Hazel needed to share this with Daniel because she thought he might help. Sometimes, all it takes is for someone to say an innocuous thing but it ends up helping immensely.

Daniel was already there, smoking a cigarette outside The Locale. The thought hadn't crossed her mind when she chose the location, but the blue façade reminded her of the painting, so

Hazel did what she did best which was to push it into a corner of her mind. He was cheerful as per usual and looked healthy and well-rested; his skin tan and his dark hair slightly grown out. Whenever Hazel thought about it, it amazed her to see how much he'd changed from the shy and skinny boy she had known in school. She wondered if she had undergone the same transformation. Daniel hugged her tightly and that already lessened her anxiety. By the time they found a table, ordered their drinks and had their first sip, Hazel almost felt like everything was back to normal again. She had simply been by herself too much, had been too focused on her thoughts.

'I have so many stories to tell you about Florence,' Daniel said, smiling without a care in the world. 'We had a wild time even trying to get there.'

'Trust me, whatever you tell me will not top the last couple of days I've had,' Hazel was convinced this was true.

'You've intrigued me now. To be fair, most of the stories from our trip come from us having to go city to city before we even got to Florence because the train we booked was cancelled and that led to a whole host of issues. I think we saw half of Italy before we got to where we were going.'

'That actually sounds like a great adventure,' Hazel felt a pang of envy because she wished she had someone to go on an adventure with, however inconvenient the adventure itself may be.

'It was, but I want to hear about your thing first. Is it to do with James?'

'What? No, why would it be?'

'Oh sorry, I just thought since it was your birthday he might have gotten in touch. My mistake.' Daniel looked embarrassed, as though he knew he should not have even mentioned his name but it was too late to take it back.

'No, this is something completely bizarre. When I was in Stockholm I went to this art gallery,'

'You never go to art galleries!'

'I know! Which is what makes this even weirder. I saw these amazing paintings by this artist who was into spirituality and I bought postcards of them, right? Except I could only buy nine postcards and there were ten paintings there. They just didn't sell the last one as a postcard for some reason. And now it's haunting me.'

'What is? The fact that you didn't buy the postcard?'

'No, the actual postcard itself. It just keeps showing up everywhere. I received it in the mail, I found it in a café, I found it at home under a cupboard. I might be going insane or I might be experiencing something supernatural.'

'Hazel, dear, I think you might need some time off or something.' Daniel was smiling, he thought it was a joke or maybe he was too nervous to believe it was real.

'I'm telling you, it's actually happening and I don't know what I'm supposed to do about it.'

'Are you sure you're not just putting the postcards there yourself?'

'I genuinely thought about it but no, I don't think I am.' They were both silent for a moment. She could tell Daniel was worried, that he was a phone call away from sectioning her. She didn't know how to prove this was true, she had nothing to substantiate it.

'This birthday, my thirty-fifth, that's how old my mum was when she,' Hazel stopped. She always had trouble saying it. She rarely had to though. People always understood without her actually having to say the words so why should she. She saw

Daniel tilt his head slightly, as if to say I'm sorry, to express his sympathy. 'I think it might be linked. I think she might be trying to tell me something.'

'You know me, I'm a big fan of the idea that there is something more out there. That there might be a way for us to communicate with the other side. I just never thought I'd actually be confronted with the idea in real life,' Daniel sighed as though he was about to say something that would disappoint her. 'I hope your mum is trying to get in touch with you. I hope this is real, Hazel.' There was something else he wanted to say but stopped himself before he did. Hazel could feel it and even though she felt happy that he could somehow see this was a possibility, she nevertheless no longer wanted to talk about it. That guilty feeling was creeping in, the one that tells you that you have overshared, said something that should have remained private.

When Hazel steered him back towards the topic of Florence, everything seemed to go back to the way it was. She laughed at his misfortunes and he showed her a few photos of the gorgeous places he'd seen. They exchanged birthday gifts and, obviously, he had bought her books as well. It was as though that conversation had not happened. It had been inconvenient, difficult to hear, and because of that Daniel found it easier to pretend it had never occurred and Hazel was fine with that because she realised she would find it difficult, if the roles were reversed, to say the right thing too. They parted outside the pub and Hazel was soon waiting for a train on a freezing platform at Glasgow Central. The wind was picking up again. There were only a few other people scattered around the platform. Hazel sat down on one of the benches and pulled the sleeves of her sweater down over her hands. To keep her mind occupied while she waited in the cold, she had a look at the booksDaniel had bought her and was happy to see that he had browsed her 'Want to Read' list on Goodreads. When she was almost done flipping through *The Magus* by John Fowles, Hazel suddenly shut the book. It took her a moment before she opened it again to the place where it was bookmarked with the missing postcard. There was a sentence that jumped out at her on the page, as if it was underlined. *'Between skin and skin, there is only light.'* Hazel looked at the postcard again, at the overlapping circles, and for some reason she wanted to cry.

*

It was close to six in the morning when Hazel woke up, jolted awake by whatever dream she had had, forgotten instantly. The night had been such a blur. She remembered leaving the book there on the platform bench, as if it was an act of rebellion, although it was mostly her going back to her old coping mechanism of denial. She had also been slightly tipsy from the drinks earlier so she had not really been sure about what she was doing. Now, Hazel had a whole day ahead of her with nothing to do and nowhere to go. Sometimes it was better this way but only if she found the right distraction that kept her occupied for long enough, her mind focused on something other than her thoughts, especially with everything that was going on at the moment. She fed Toffee, made some builder's tea and the cat soon joined her on the sofa where they were going to spend the rest of their day watching *Grey's Anatomy,* her ultimate comfort show that required no mental exertion. Hazel was about to turn on the TV when she heard the metal clink of her mail slot. The sound of air being disturbed. The soft swoosh as something landed on the carpet of her entryway. She wanted to ignore it, wholeheartedly, but she couldn't. She stared at the ceiling for a while, blinking away the tears that were threatening to form. Then, carrying Toffee in her arms, hugging him close, she went to retrieve the postcard and then went back to her sofa. She sat down and stared at it. Hazel knew she had never looked at something so intensely. She tried to examine each detail, pay attention to each tiny brushstroke she could notice in this small format, tried her hardest to understand what it was trying to tell her. When she looked up again, it was hours later. It was no longer dawn and the street outside was now busy and obscured by a rain shower.

Rain was falling heavily, creating a wall in front of her. At times, the wind would break the wall and send the droplets against her face, the cold water stinging her skin. Hazel thought that didn't know where she was going but once she got to the entrance to Lambhill cemetery she realised this had been her destination all along. She strayed off the path, slipping on the mud, not even caring if she fell, stumbling amongst the headstones, trying to find a place she had tried to forget. Once she reached her mum's grave, she felt a sharp stabbing in her chest. She noticed how exhausted she was, how much all of this had weighed on her. She had avoided this place for years. When she was younger, Hazel used to come here with her dad to clean up the grave, put down some flowers but once it stopped being a routine, she could not face it alone. Even when she had been here with her dad, they had just stood by the grave, not saying anything. Hazel had felt incapable of conveying any emotion because she had not known what the right emotion was. For years she had been upset about what had happened but had never addressed how it made her feel apart from that. She was soaked through and shivering, the rain showing no signs of stopping. Hazel wanted to scream but nothing was coming out. Even at the height of her frustration, she was unable to break that barrier of normality and shyness. She fell to her knees and placed her head against the stone slab. This was as close to hugging her mum as she had come since that last day. How much had happened since then; all the stories she could have shared with her, the heartbreaks, the silly moments, her accomplishments. The joy of being in the same time and place as her mum would have changed things.

'Was it you?' Hazel asked her.

Just then, she could swear that she heard an answer. A whisper in her ear or maybe a voice inside her mind, if she was going crazy, she wasn't sure. A plea but also an invitation to let go. The voice asking Hazel to stop holding on to hate. She hadn't realised she had any hate in her heart but that's only because she had buried it so deeply, hanging on to it as if it were treasure instead of something poisonous. Ever since it happened, everyone around her had just assumed that she was sad and so Hazel herself assumed that this was how she felt. There had been more to it and she had never even realised. Hazel could feel the moment when she let it go, it was as if she had another pair of hands inside her clutching that emotion, clasping it so tightly that her entire body was tense from the effort, and then suddenly, everything just became soft and she could finally breathe without having to catch her breath from the strain of it all. Hazel placed a kiss on her mother's grave and stood up. She wiped away her tears and slowly began her walk back home. It was already getting dark and she was so tired that she was sure she would fall asleep instantly. But she knew that this sleep would be different. It would be the first time in a long time that she would truly rest.